NEEDING ARELLA

TERRI ANNE BROWNING

Copyright © Terri Anne Browning/Anna Henson 2020

All rights reserved. No part of this publication may be reproduced, distributed, or transmitted in any form or by any means, or stored in a database or retrieval system, without the prior written permission of Terri Anne Browning, except as permitted under the US Copyright Act of 1976.

Needing Arella

Rockers' Legacy Book 6

Written by Terri Anne Browning

All Rights Reserved ©Terri Anne Browning 2020

Cover Design Sara Eirew Photography

Edited by Lisa Hollett of Silently Correcting Your Grammar

10 9 8 7 6 5 4 3 2 1

Needing Arella is a work of fiction. Names, characters, places, and incidents are the products of the author's imagination or are used fictitiously. Any resemblance to actual events, locales, or persons, living or dead, is entirely coincidental.

No part of this book can be reproduced in any form by electronic or mechanical means, including storage or retrieval systems, without the express permission in writing from the author. The only exception is by a reviewer who may quote short excerpts in a review.

FAMILY TREE: ROCKERS

Emmie & Nik: Mia (Barrick—Emerson), Jagger (Shaw)

Jesse & Layla: Lucy (Harris—Hayat and Evan), Luca (Violet—Remi, aka Love Bug), Lyric (Mila—Ian and Isaac)

Drake & Lana: Nevaeh (Braxton—Conrad), Arella, Heavenleigh, Bliss, Damian

Shane & Harper: Violet (Luca—Remi, aka Love Bug), Mason

Axton & Dallas: Kenzie (Bishop—Knox and Vera), Cannon, Shaw (Jagger)

Wroth & Marissa: Jackson, Bryant, Liam, Dorothy/Doe

Devlin & Natalie: Harris (Lucy—Hayat and Evan), Trinity

Liam & Gabriella: Asher, Piper

Zander & Annabelle: Michelle, Mieke (Kaden—Michelle and Nash), Jaco

Linc & Rhett: Lennon, Ripley

Jenna & Angie: Iris, Morgana

Siblings

Drake, Shane, Natalie, Jenna

Layla, Lana, Lucy
Liam, Marissa

FAMILY TREE: MC

Raven & Bash: Lexa (Ben—Finn), Max
 Spider & Willa: Maverick, Mila (Lyric—Isaac and Ian), Monroe (Gian—Gianna and Lillianna)
 Hawk & Gracie: Jack
 Jet & Flick: Garret, Nova
 Raider & Quinn: Kingston
 Matt & Rory: Chance
 Colt & Kelli: River
 Tanner & Jos: Reid, Elias
 Siblings
 Jet, Hawk, Raider, Colt, Raven
 Tanner, Matt

FAMILY TREE: MAFIA

Scarlett & Ciro: Zayne, Zariah, Ciana, Vito, Benito

Victoria & Adrian: Theo (Tavia), Sofia

Allegra & Dante: Jenny, Adley, Mateo

Cristiano & Anya: Ryan, Samara

Siblings
    Cristiano, Scarlett, Victoria
    Adrian, Anya

TIMELINE READING ORDER FOR THE ROCKER...UNIVERSE

Our Broken Love Collection (Alexis)
- The Rocker Who Holds Me
- The Rocker Who Savors Me
- The Rocker Who Needs Me
- The Rocker Who Loves Me
- The Rocker Who Holds Her
- The Rockers' Babies
- Angel's Halo
- Angel's Halo Entangled
- Angel's Halo Guardian Angel
- The Rocker Who Wants Me
- The Rocker Who Cherishes Me
- The Rocker Who Shatters Me
- The Rocker Who Hates Me
- Angel's Halo Reclaimed
- The Rocker Who Betrays Me
- Defying Her Mafioso
- His Mafioso Princess
- Angel's Halo Atonement
- Angel's Halo Fallen Angel

Marrying Her Mafioso
Angel's Halo Avenged
Her Mafioso King
Angel's Halo Forever Angel
Forever Rockers
Needing Forever Vol 1
Catching Lucy
Craving Lucy
Rocking Kin
Un-Shattering Lucy
Needing the Memories
Tainted Kiss
Tainted Butterfly
Forever Lucy
Tainted Bastard
Tainted Heartbreak
Tainted Forever
Needing Forever Vol 2
Salvation
Holding Mia
Needing Nevaeh
Off-Limits
Sweet Agony
Savoring Mila
Surviving His Scars
Loving Violet
Wanting Shaw
Needing Arella
Sacred Vow (Maverick & River)
Her Shelter (Max)

PROLOGUE
ARELLA

The laughter and voices in the room were like a dull roar, with everyone I loved filling the house.

Well, almost everyone. There was still one person missing. With each minute that passed, the knot in my gut tightened, making me feel like my middle was being squeezed in half.

He was okay, I tried to assure myself. Jordan was just running late. He wanted to surprise me, make me think he wasn't coming, and then when he showed up, I would have the biggest smile on my face. Just for him. He would sweep me off my feet, and we would have our happily ever after.

It wasn't wishful thinking. I'd seen it happen right in front of my eyes with my sister Nevaeh and her husband, Braxton. He'd shown up at her own eighteenth birthday party, and their entire relationship had been like a fairy tale ever since. Sure, there had been one or two bumps along the way, but that had only strengthened their love for each other.

I'd only been sixteen at the time, but I knew it would

happen for me with Jordan. Our chemistry couldn't be ignored any longer. The last time we'd hung out, just the day before, the air around us had felt charged. The hunger I'd seen in his eyes had matched my own; the way he'd had to stop himself from touching me time and time again had left me trembling by the time he'd said goodnight.

His face had been tense as I'd stood beside his car with him, silently begging him to kiss me. There had been only a few short hours left until I turned the magical eighteen. One kiss wouldn't have hurt anything. But he'd only stroked the backs of his fingers down my cheek and given me a tight smile before telling me goodnight.

I hadn't reminded him about my party. We'd talked about it earlier in the night, before watching a movie in the living room, so I knew he would remember. Plus, I didn't want to sound desperate and annoying. Girls like that always made me roll my eyes, but I was starting to get why they did those things. They were just so infatuated—so in love—they couldn't help themselves.

But just because I felt like I couldn't breathe without him with each day that passed and I wasn't officially his, didn't mean I was going to turn into someone I wasn't. That was insane.

Right?

My eyes were trained on the front door, so when it opened, I held my breath. Only for it to be pushed out forcefully when I saw it wasn't Jordan Moreitti, but his parents instead.

I blinked at the beautiful couple, who were both welcomed by my mother and then Aunt Emmie. Alexis Moreitti held one small present in her hand, while the other clutched her cane. Her husband stood at her side, his eyes adoring her as she spoke to the two women in front of them, but I noticed he, too, was carrying a small gift.

The knot in my stomach tightened more and more, and I pulled out my phone, making sure yet again that I hadn't missed a text or call from him. But the screen was empty. I swallowed the lump in my throat and put on a brave smile, somehow knowing in my heart that Jordan wasn't coming.

Maybe he was sick.

Why else would he not show up on this day, of all days? My eighteenth birthday was a big deal. Not only was I officially an adult, but it meant that we could finally be together. Even though we'd been hanging out so much over the past two years as just friends, I'd made no secret of the fact that I wanted more. Everyone in my family knew how I felt about him, especially Jordan's best friend, Mia.

As I stood there, I watched Mia walk over to the Moreittis, with her beautiful baby daughter on her hip. She embraced Alexis, and Emerson gave a sweet giggle when Jared Moreitti bent his knees to speak directly to the toddler.

I shouldn't have been so jealous that Mia was close with Jordan's family. She was his best friend after all. They thought of her as a daughter and had even included her in family gatherings all her life. Of course they adored her and would treat Emerson as if she were their very own granddaughter.

But that didn't kill the jealousy that ate me up inside whenever I thought about Mia and Jordan. I hated that they were best friends, that the two of them were still so close. Maybe I wouldn't have felt like that if I didn't know they had slept together in the past. Then again, maybe I would.

Was it so crazy that I wanted to be Jordan's best friend?

That I wanted to be included in his family like Mia so easily was?

Instead, his parents shot me a glance that told me they weren't comfortable approaching me on their own. I couldn't really blame them. Jordan had never taken me to their house or even invited me to share a meal with his parents. I knew them only because they sometimes came to parties, usually those hosted by Aunt Emmie, like her famous Christmas Eve party. To them, I was just one of Emmie Armstrong's nieces. If I was lucky, they might even think of me as one of their son's friends, but I doubted they would ever consider me more to either Jordan or themselves.

Especially since he was apparently blowing off my birthday party.

I quickly pushed that thought down, not wanting to get angry if he was, in fact, sick. With presents in hand, they had obviously come in Jordan's place. And he wouldn't miss my birthday unless he were ill or it was important.

"Arella," Palmer murmured from beside me. I turned my gaze away from the couple staring uncomfortably in my direction and glanced at my best friend. Palmer looked at me with concern as she touched the back of her hand to my forehead. "Are you feeling okay? You went pale all of a sudden."

I forced a smile, but she knew me so well that she could tell it didn't reach my eyes. "Just a little tired, I guess. My mom and sisters took me out shopping all day, then we spent a few hours at my favorite spa."

I'd been pampered to within an inch of my life with first a massage and then had my hair and nails done. It felt like I was getting ready for prom or the red carpet when someone started doing my makeup. But for me, it was so much more than that. Today was supposed to be one of the most important and life-changing days of my existence.

Only it wasn't turning out anything like I expected.

I could tell by the look in Palmer's brown eyes she wasn't buying what I was selling, but she didn't call me out on it. She glanced over my shoulder, and I knew she was looking at the Moreittis. Grasping my hand, she gave it a firm squeeze. "Here they come with your mom," she said. "Give me that killer smile of yours and giggle like you mean it."

I did just that without questioning her, knowing she would never steer me wrong. I felt a few eyes on me as I giggled, filling the room with the singsong sound that always made my dad smile, no matter what. Moments later, Mom murmured my name, and I turned to find her standing behind me with the Moreittis at her side.

I widened my eyes in surprise, thankful for all the acting classes I'd taken over the years. "Mr. and Mrs. Moreitti," I greeted. "It's so nice to see you."

Alexis gave me a small but warm smile. "Happy birthday, sweetheart." She offered me the gift in her hand. "Just a little something from us."

"Thank you," I told her sincerely. "You didn't have to do that. Just having you here means so much."

Her face softened somewhat, some of the tension leaving her shoulders. "We also wanted to deliver Jordan's present in person." She glanced up at her husband, and he handed over the present he was holding on to.

"Jordan had to make a quick trip to Italy for me," he said with a grim smile. "He regrets he couldn't make it in person, but he made us promise to give you this personally."

I stared down at the small box wrapped in metallic red paper with a glittery red bow on top. Metallic red was my favorite color, something Jordan knew. But the gift his mother had given me was wrapped identically, and for some reason, that made me feel like crying.

When I made no move to take the present from him, Palmer saved me. "Why don't I hold this while you unwrap the Moreittis' present?" she murmured.

I put on my best smile, which put the Moreittis at ease, but it didn't fool either Palmer or my mom, who was giving me a concerned frown. I forced my fingers not to tremble as I carefully unwrapped their small present and found a gift card to one of my favorite boutiques. It was a thoughtful gift but impersonal, and it told me they hadn't wasted much energy putting effort into it.

Still, I was thankful for it, and I told them so as I hugged them both.

When they glanced at Palmer, still holding Jordan's gift, I discreetly shot Mom a "Help me" look. Without question, she turned to the Moreittis with a beaming smile. "Oh, look! There's Drake. Gabriella was telling us just last week how active you two are with GreenPlanet. Did you know they asked him to do a single just for their latest fundraiser?"

Their eyes brightened, and they let Mom lead them over to my dad. Once they were out of earshot, Palmer glared down at the present still in her hands. "What should I do with this?"

The smile I'd kept in place for Jordan's parents vanished. When I looked at his gift, all I wanted to do was cry. His dad wasn't very convincing about the work excuse, so I didn't believe it for a second. Still, I couldn't bring myself to throw away anything Jordan gave me.

I took the small box. "I'm just going to put this in my room," I told her as I started for the stairs. "I won't be long."

Upstairs, I closed and locked my door before falling back against it. Tears burned my eyes, and I clenched my fingers around the shiny present so hard they quickly began to ache. Fighting a sob, I moved on shaking legs to the bed and flopped inelegantly down on the end.

Pushing my hair back from my face, I tossed the box on my pillow and then pulled out my phone. Heart racing, I hit a hashtag search on social media, and instantly, a hundred pictures appeared. The first one was time-stamped within the last ten minutes.

Jordan was in a suit, but his white dress shirt was half unbuttoned, his tie barely hanging around his neck. There was red lipstick on his shirt collar. That same shade was smeared over his mouth as well as his cheek and neck. Whoever took the picture had a good angle, because I could see the drunken look in Jordan's dark eyes.

Beside him, some redhead hid her head in his chest, but the side of her face was still visible, and I could see she was grinning. The post that went with the pictures said Jordan and his date—Letizia, some Italian celebrity heiress —were leaving Milan's hottest club. They got into Letizia's limo. There were already over a hundred replies to the tweet, and one said they saw the couple getting out of the limo in front of Letizia's villa. The time stamp was less than a minute before.

I quickly did the math in my head. Milan was nine hours ahead of California. That meant it was just after four in the morning there.

As I was doing the calculation, a new picture came up to go with the tweet, showing Jordan and Letizia passionately making out in front of the small but beautiful Italian villa.

Pain exploded in my chest, and it took me a few minutes before I could breathe again.

I swallowed the lump clogging my throat and turned off my phone. As I tossed it onto my bedside table, my gaze landed on Jordan's present, and I let a single tear fall.

There would be no fairy tale for me. The man I'd loved and waited for wasn't going to sweep me off my feet. While I'd been unrealistically building up what I was feeling for Jordan in my head—and my heart—he hadn't been doing the same. I should have known better. Nevaeh, who was the smartest person I'd ever met, had tried to warn me from the very beginning. But I hadn't listened.

I thought since Dad had fallen for and waited for Mom until she was eighteen, and the same had happened with Nevi and Brax, that it meant it would be my destiny too. Only, while I was falling head over heels for my Prince Charming, he'd just thought of me as a friend.

And not even his best friend.

That was reserved for Mia.

The pain in my heart and stomach only intensified. Hadn't that Letizia chick looked a lot like Mia? What little I saw of her in those two pictures with her red hair and fair skin, she did resemble my cousin somewhat.

I pressed my hand to my chest, trying to rub the pain away. Of course he went for girls who looked like Mia. He was in love with her. I'd suspected it for years, but I hadn't wanted to believe it.

Now, I had no choice but to.

"Stupid, stupid girl," I whispered to myself, angrily scrubbing the single teardrop away. "You had no business falling for him to begin with."

I drew in a slow, steadying breath and stood. Locking my knees to keep them from trembling, I walked to my full-length mirror and glared at the girl staring back at me. "You will not love him anymore. Jordan Moreitti is nothing more than your friend. You don't need him. You won't cry over him. You won't even think about him."

Walking back to my bed, I picked up the unwrapped gift and then placed it at the back of my closet, locking it away along with the key to my heart.

SEVEN MONTHS **Later**
Jordan

Lana Stevenson's soft sobs were so heartbreaking that no one was left unaffected. She clung to her husband, burying her face in his chest as the minister said the last prayer. The beautiful woman was surrounded by her children, sisters, and other family members, but she was so distraught she couldn't see anything but the casket that held her father.

It was closed, with white roses on top along with a picture of Cole surrounded by his daughter and all five of his grandchildren. The smile on the old rocker's face was possibly the most genuine the man had ever had. His happiness seemed to shine out of his eyes and glow around the seven people in the picture as the afternoon sun gleamed down on the silver frame.

But neither Lana's heart-wrenching sobs nor the picture could hold my attention. Not when *she* was only a few yards away.

I stared across the open grave at the girl who had been tormenting me night and day from the time she was barely sixteen fucking years old. At times, I was disgusted with myself and how easily Arella Stevenson could twist my thoughts of her into something dirty and sexual.

The age gap between us might have been considered minuscule compared to the one between her parents, but since she'd been so young when I'd first started having those filthy fantasies about her, it made me feel like a lecherous old man.

But that hadn't stopped me from seeking out her attention. From obsessing about her every move. Or from aching for just a smile from the beauty who haunted me even when I was halfway around the world and deep between someone else's thighs.

It hadn't worked, though. I couldn't fuck her out of my system with other women, and eventually, I just gave up trying to make the ache go away with random hookups. Because no matter how many other girls I'd fucked, none of them could make me feel the peace that Arella could with just the brush of her fingertips down my jaw.

And now she stood in tears as the world said its final goodbye to her grandfather.

Cole Steel had passed in his sleep days before. The paps had gone crazy with the story, spouting bullshit like they found him facedown in some pornstars's pussy, coked out of his head. They claimed he'd overdosed and that was why his heart had stopped.

The truth wasn't nearly as dramatic, from what Mia had shared when she'd called to tell me about Cole's passing.

Cole had had a heart attack, but he was too stubborn to seek medical attention. Instead, he'd thought he could just ignore the pain the pain and passed in his sleep. His daughter had found him the next morning when she and Drake showed up, determined to make him go to the doctor.

I'd been in Milan when my best friend called to tell me

about his death, and the first thing I could think about was how distraught Arella must be. She was close to the old rocker, whom she so affectionately called "Pop-Pop," so I knew she had to be hurting. As soon as I hung up with Mia, I'd tried to call her, but her phone was off.

I'd attempted again and again on the trip home, but her phone remained off the entire time. I hadn't gotten back until late the night before, and even though I'd wanted to drive straight to her parents' house to check on her, I knew I would see her today and I forced myself to go to my apartment.

During the church service, Arella had been surrounded by her parents and siblings, so I hadn't been able to get close to her. I tightened my hands into fists as she shifted beside her older sister and best friend. She lifted her gaze from the casket that was now being lowered into the ground, finally locking her eyes with mine.

Her blue-gray eyes were full of so much pain, I felt something twist in my chest. It was torture to see her with tears in her beautiful eyes, with her face so tense and pale. I ached to pull her into my arms and just hold her. I would have gladly given her every ounce of strength I had to get her through such a tragic time.

Finally, the last prayer was finished, and the graveside service concluded. Around her, everyone slowly started to return to their limos, but Arella just stood there, seeming frozen in place while her eyes stayed glued to me.

Vaguely, I heard Mia murmur that she and Barrick would see me at the Stevensons', where everyone was going to show their respects and have a meal in Cole's honor. Her words barely registered as I moved in the opposite direction.

When I reached Arella, I wasted no time and pulled her into my arms. She was stiff at first, her entire body rigid against me until I kissed the top of her head. Then, one by one, her muscles began to relax, and she sank into me, wrapping her arms around my middle and clinging to me.

I felt her begin to tremble, and then a soft sob left her, making me tighten my hold around her. "Baby, it's okay. I have you."

"I can't believe he's gone," she cried into my chest. "I miss him so much."

I pressed my lips to her temple, breathing in the sweet scent of her shampoo, and I closed my eyes as I fought my own sting of tears. Her pain was pressing down on me like a weight, making her agony feel as if it were my own.

"Arella," a deep voice spoke from behind her, and I lifted my eyes to find her father standing only a few feet away. Drake Stevenson's eyes drilled into me hard, his jaw clenched.

For the past few years, he'd welcomed me into his home and accepted my friendship with his second-oldest daughter without so much as a blink. But I got the sudden vibe that he wanted to bury me right along with his father-in-law. Instinctively, I tightened my arms around Arella, fearing he wanted to take her away from me.

Arella lifted her head and, with another sob, pulled away from me and threw herself into his arms. He tucked her against him and, without a word to me, walked her toward the limo where her mother and siblings were already waiting.

As I stood there, watching her walk away without a backward glance, I felt a void in the center of my chest that left me breathless. Gritting my teeth, I returned to my car and drove to the Stevensons' house in Santa Monica.

By the time I got there, the driveway was already overflowing, and other vehicles were lined up along the street.

For several minutes I just sat there, my fingers so tight around the wheel, they were bloodless.

Honestly, I wasn't even sure why I'd rushed back when Mia informed me of Cole's passing. I'd barely known the man. But the thought of Arella hurting had driven me mental. That girl had a hold on me, and I didn't know how to break it.

Or if I even wanted to.

I'd been fighting myself for years, but back then, her age had been enough for me to keep my hands to myself. Now, she was eighteen. There was nothing to stand in my way if I decided to explore what I felt for her. I knew she felt the same, and if I was honest, that was why I'd agreed to go back to Italy when my father had needed someone to take care of a project that required "special" attention.

Letizia was a spoiled little bitch, but I'd taken care of business and then gotten pulled into her drama on top of it. The gossip rags had been printing bullshit about the two of us ever since. Not all of it was lies, but there was just enough of the truth included in their articles about the two of us to make it believable. The publicity was sufficient to keep my father's PR people busy, and so far, shareholders were pleased with my handling of the "project," so I hadn't made any of those idiotic trash magazines retract anything.

Yet.

My patience was wearing thin where Letizia was concerned, however, and I wanted to be done with this stupid assignment so I could get home—and yes, possibly explore what Arella and I could have, if given a chance.

Eventually, I unlocked my fingers and walked up the driveway to the front door. As I did, I noticed another vehicle parking, and I glanced over. Several guys I didn't recognize in dress slacks and button-up shirts exited the

SUV. I heard one of them say Arella's name, and I gritted my teeth as jealousy hit me dead center in the gut.

Angrily, I hit the doorbell, and moments later, Braxton Collins opened the door. He gave me a dispassionate once-over before stepping back. "Figured you would have been on a plane by now."

"My flight isn't until early tomorrow," I informed him as I stepped into the huge house. I probably shouldn't even have taken the time to come home for this funeral, but I'd dropped everything and rushed to get back to my girl.

Gritting my teeth, I reminded myself that she wasn't "my girl" yet. I needed to take care of work first, and then I could come back and make her mine.

I'd been to the Stevensons' home plenty of times in the past to hang out with Arella, but after that look Drake Stevenson had given me earlier, I wasn't sure if I was going to be so openly welcomed any longer. I didn't know what that was about, but it made my gut clench that maybe I'd fucked up in a major way.

Braxton started to close the door just as the guys from the SUV walked up onto the porch. Hearing their voices, Arella's brother-in-law jerked the door open once again then sighed in annoyance. "You idiots again," he muttered but stepped back.

"Hey, man," the guy I'd heard speak Arella's name greeted. "How's my girl holding up?"

I fisted my hands at my sides. What the fuck had he just said? No fucking way he'd called *my* girl his.

Trying to temper my anger and jealousy, I found myself blinking at the douchebag who was still talking. He was tall, but a few inches shorter than me. His shoulders were on the leaner side of muscular, but there was a cockiness to him that made him seem larger than he really was. His chiseled jaw, high cheekbones, and the cocky tilt to his chin made me want to put a fist through his pretty face.

"Braxton, honey, is everything...okay?" Arella's mom's voice drifted off as her honey-brown eyes landed on me. Her lips pressed into a hard line, reinforcing my trepidation that I'd screwed up somehow, before her gaze traveled to the other guys still standing in the doorway. "Hi, Lyle...and Lyle's friends." She gave a grim smile. "Well, Arella will be glad to see all your handsome faces. Please come in. She's helping out in the kitchen right now if you want to grab something to snack on."

Lyle took a moment to kiss her cheek. "Thanks, Mrs. Stevenson. I'm really sorry about your dad. He was a cool guy."

Lana's chin trembled for a moment before she forced it to stop. "He was," she agreed in a choked voice. Clearing her throat, she waved her hand. "Please make yourselves at home."

When they took a step toward the kitchen, I moved faster, feeling a desperate need to reach Arella before Lyle did.

I heard her voice before I even reached the kitchen door. The soft, almost musical sound that always eased something tight within me. A small laugh reached my ears, and I ached to wrap my fingers around that sound so I could always hold on to it.

Entering the kitchen, I found Arella and all three of her sisters helping the caterers set up a buffet-style lunch. Wiping her hands on a towel, Arella stood close to Nevaeh as they watched Heavenleigh and Bliss finish taking lids off of huge containers.

"Douchebag at two o'clock," Heavenleigh muttered, and her older sisters turned in my direction.

Nevaeh's blue-gray eyes landed on me from behind a pair of glasses that took up most of her face and narrowed. I barely met her gaze before turning straight back to Arella. She'd changed from the simple, knee-length black dress she'd worn to the funeral into a pair of jean shorts and a Steel Entrapment T-shirt, no doubt in honor of her grandfather since he'd been the front man and founder of the band.

Her long dark hair, which had been in soft waves at the funeral, was pulled into a ponytail that showed off her elegant neck and that damn mole that had always fascinated me, located where her neck and shoulder connected. I'd fantasized about licking it—sinking my teeth into her flesh and marking her so that no one could see it and not know that she was mine.

"Mia's in the living room," Bliss announced, causing Arella to flinch and glance at her youngest sister.

Ignoring the youngest Stevenson in the room, I crossed the kitchen to Arella. "Can we talk?"

"Um..." Her hesitation only made me tense more, and then Lyle and his idiot friends walked in. Her gaze left me, landed on him, and I saw something flash in her blue-grays that made me want to destroy Lyle. "Hey, you," she greeted, walking around me and hugging the guy. "I wasn't expecting you until later."

He wrapped his arms around her and kissed her forehead as his gaze locked with mine over her head. "I couldn't stay away." Leaning back, he focused on her. "How are you holding up?"

"Better now that you're here." She linked her arm through his and turned for the door, completely ignoring me. "Everything is ready to go in here. Let me tell Daddy I'm leaving, and we can go pick up Palmer."

"We don't have to leave. I know this is a family time."

"No, no," she rushed to assure him as they left the room, his friends right behind them. "My parents know I need some time with you and my friends."

Feeling gut-punched, I just stood there, watching her walk away.

What the fuck just happened?

Did I...lose her?

ONE
ARELLA

THE CUTE BARISTA HANDED OVER MY LATTE WITH A wink, and I blew him a kiss as I turned to exit the coffee shop. Heath was nothing but a flirt, but he knew how to make the best latte in all of SoCal. He knew my order so well, he started making it as soon as I walked through the door, even though the place was packed from wall-to-wall. By the time I ordered and paid, my drink was already waiting.

A glance at the cup showed my name with a heart for the last "a," and it put a smile on my face as I walked to my car. It was an unseasonably warm day, and the top was down on the convertible my parents had given me when I'd graduated from high school, so I could enjoy the sun on my skin. The tiny white Porsche Boxster was adorable, and I loved it.

As I dropped into the driver's seat, my cell went off. Seeing it was just my best friend Palmer, I decided to let it go to voice mail and call her back later. I wanted a few moments of complete quiet while I enjoyed my coffee and drove back to the set. We'd taken an hour break for lunch and I'd done a little Christmas shopping before grabbing my coffee, so I needed to drive straight back before I was too late.

A guard gave me a chin lift when I reached the studio lot, and he waved me through without making me pause. I gave the middle-aged guy a wink as I passed him, and he grinned. After parking, I walked inside, where we were filming the latest episode of the show I starred in as one of the three lead characters, tossing my now-empty coffee cup as I headed directly for the makeup chair. This was the final season of this damn show, and honestly, I couldn't wait to be done with this character and the show itself.

I'd had to deal with people trying to trash my name and dragging me through the mud for taking this role. Apparently to the world in general, I only got the leading female role for this drama because of who my father and grandfather were. Using my name to get to the top, blocking actresses who could actually act from getting the job.

Which was why I hadn't quit when I'd realized just how much I hated this character and the other people I worked with. I wasn't about to let anyone think I was running from having them talk shit about me. I gave 110 percent to the role, despite wanting to stab nearly every person on set most days. I'd won a Golden Globe for my performance the year before, but not even that award had saved this idiotic drama when the network decided to make some cuts.

I had other jobs already lined up, so as soon as we wrapped up the show for the final episodes in February, I could take my pick of whatever role I wanted.

"Miss Stevenson, you have a package in your dressing room," Freddie, the director's assistant, informed me when he spotted me.

I gave him a small smile. Freddie was possibly the least annoying person on set, so I always tried to be nice to him. "Thanks. I'll get it later."

After I spent over an hour getting my makeup redone for the second time that day and I had to deal with the torture of putting on that stupid blond wig I hated so much, the afternoon passed in a blur of take after take. I was ready to drop by the time I made it to my dressing room. The couch by the window seemed so inviting, enticing me to lie down for an hour or two for a nap before I drove home, but I wanted the comfort of my own bed more.

I grabbed my gym bag that I brought with me every day and held all my essentials, then I spotted the medium-sized package Freddie had told me about earlier. When I picked it up, it was surprisingly lighter than I expected. A courier must have dropped it off, because I didn't see a return address, just my name and the address of the studio where my show was filmed five days a week for twenty-plus weeks of the year.

Figuring it was work-related since the director's assistant had put it in my dressing room, I decided to open it when I got home. Yawning, I walked out to my car and quickly put the top up since the temperature had dropped now that the sun was down.

Traffic sucked, so it was almost an hour later before I walked into my apartment. I dropped my bag and the box before engaging the locks and making my way into the kitchen. I had a housekeeper who came in during the week to tidy up and cook me some dinner so my mom didn't worry I wasn't eating right.

Pulling the food container out of the fridge, I saw Carol had made grilled salmon with asparagus and wild rice. I popped it into the microwave and decided to call Palmer back.

"Have you been on any of the socials today?" my best friend demanded in greeting as soon as she answered.

I grabbed a bottle of water and uncapped it, rolling my eyes. You would think she was the actress with how dramatic she could be at times. "Nope. I've been too busy to worry about social media land and everyone's shit today."

And I knew she would give me all the highlights anyway, so most of the time, I just waited for her to give me a rundown on all our mutual friends.

By the time the microwave dinged, she was still talking a mile a minute and I was a little bored with her recounting of the social media soap opera. I put her on speaker and just let her talk while I ate standing up by the sink. I didn't even hear half of what she said. I was half asleep and only wanted to fall face first into bed.

"I don't know what he sees in that bitch anyway. She's not even close to being in your realm of hotness. And have you heard her laugh? Ugh. So annoying."

The disgust in her voice made me smile, even though I didn't know who she was talking about.

"Tell us how you really feel, Palms," I laughed before taking the last bite of my dinner, and then I rinsed the plate. Licking my lips, I put it in the empty dishwasher and then grabbed one of the tiny chocolate caramel truffle balls that I indulged in for dessert most nights. I needed something sweet after dinner, but I couldn't risk gaining weight from eating the way I really wanted to. Those truffles saved my career and my thighs.

She gave a disgusted grunt. "She's so trashy, Arella. Admit it, you think so too."

"Of course she is," I agreed, still unsure who she was talking about.

"Anyway, I heard she lost her mind when he was seen out with the Danish princess or whatever she is." She gave a snort. "Now that's a hot piece of ass I'd like a taste of."

My grin was so big, it made my face hurt. I'd known Palmer was a lesbian from the time we were in middle school. She might even have had a crush on me at one point, but once she realized my heart was with Jordan, she'd moved on. She'd never made her sexual orientation a secret to me, but she hadn't come out to anyone else, especially not her judgmental mother. I wasn't a fan of Veronica Abbot, but her husband, Trent, was pretty cool. I knew he wouldn't disown his daughter if she came out to him. Veronica, on the other hand, would lose her mind.

"The redhead or the blonde?" I asked, trying to picture which Danish princess she was talking about.

"The redhead, duh," she scoffed. "Jordan is all about redheads, and we both know why. You've said so many times that he's secretly in love with Mia. I mean, Letizia even has that pretty dark-red hair. It's about the only thing pretty about her, if you ask me."

Suddenly, my dinner and the truffle were no longer sitting happily in my stomach. Of course she was talking about Jordan and Letizia. My tired brain hadn't put it together, but now that I knew who she was talking about, I wanted to hit rewind and not even have called Palmer back.

I didn't want to think about Jordan Moreitti or any of the redheads he'd been blowing up social media and the trash mags with over the past few years. He was my friend, and we still hung out on occasion, but ever since my eighteenth birthday, our once-close relationship had disappeared.

It was annoying, because most of my extended family assumed that just because I went out to dinner or a movie every now and then with Jordan that I was waiting with bated breath for him to come to his senses and be with me. The truth was, I'd moved on the day after my eighteenth birthday. Jordan was nothing more than a friend, and that was the way it was going to stay.

There was no fucking way I was going to ever give him that kind of power over my heart again.

Even though I didn't trust him with my heart, he was still fun to be around. When we hung out, he gave me his full attention. But I knew as soon as I was out of sight, I was very much out of his mind. He'd been fucking Letizia on and off for the past year or so, from what I could tell through social media. We never talked about his sex life, though. I doubt I could have stomached hearing all about the women he warmed his bed with.

The redheaded chicks who all looked eerily like Mia.

Holding back a sigh, I listened to Palmer talk shit about Letizia and then spout a few sonnets about the Danish princess's amazing ass before I told my best friend that I needed a shower and my pillow.

My heart felt heavy as I ended the call. On my way to my room, I had to pass the front door. Seeing the box I had yet to open, I picked it up and carried it into my bedroom with me. Setting it on the end of my bed, I grabbed the pair of scissors out of my nightstand and sliced through the tape.

Fighting a yawn, I lifted the flaps and was annoyed when I found a crap-ton of packing peanuts on top. "Really?" I groused. "What is even in here?"

I grabbed the wastebasket beside my small desk by the window and brought it back before emptying most of the little Styrofoam balls into it. Once it was clear enough that I could see what was inside, I was surprised it wasn't something small and fragile considering how many packing peanuts had been in the box.

Instead, it held a bottle of my favorite lotion with an envelope with my name scrawled across the front. Smiling at the thoughtfulness of whoever had sent me the rose-scented lotion, I picked it up. I loved this stuff, and I'd been out for the past few weeks. But with Christmas coming up, I knew at least one of my sisters or my mom would get me some as a present because they all knew how much I loved it.

My smile dimmed when I felt how light the large bottle was. At least half the contents were gone, but I didn't see any spilled inside the box. "Someone really sent me a half-full bottle of lotion?" I muttered to myself as I rolled my eyes.

Tossing the bottle onto the bed beside the box, I picked up the large envelope. It was at least 9 x 12, so I figured it held a document that needed my attention. Wondering if it was from my agent, I lifted the flap. As my fingers slid over the glossy top page, I realized it was actually photos and pulled them out.

"Holy shit," I whispered when my gaze landed on the first picture. Bile lifted into my throat as my brain tried to block out what I was seeing.

It was obviously a guy in the picture, although all that was showing was the lower half of his body. His naked lower body. In one hand, he held the bottle of rose-scented lotion, the other one must have held the camera he took the picture with.

Unable to stop myself, I flipped through the next few pictures. The second photo showed him squirting a huge glob of lotion down his shaft. In the third, he was stroking himself, massaging the creaminess into his slightly above-average member.

Fingers shaking, I pulled the last picture free from the stack and saw that he'd obviously made himself come. The mess was on his thighs and lower abdomen. Sickened by it all, I dropped the pictures at my feet.

As they landed, the last picture fell facedown, and I realized something was written on the back of it.

I can't wait to rub this all over your sweet body, little bird.

"Shit, shit, shit," I whisper-shouted and ran for the bathroom.

Just the thought of the guy in those pictures touching me made me sick, and I dropped to my knees in the nick of time to empty my stomach into the toilet.

When I was face-to-face with my entire dinner once again, I flushed and then dropped down so that my back was pressed against the sink cabinet. I felt drained and still nauseated. Reluctantly, I looked into my bedroom, as if those damn pictures could see me, and fought a shudder.

I received inappropriate fan mail all the time. It was part of being famous. But I'd never gotten something like... that. It was disgusting—and creepy.

And scary.

I started to shiver so hard my teeth began to chatter. My first thought was to take a hot shower to warm up, but the thought of being naked while those pictures were only yards away made me feel too exposed.

First things first. I needed to get those damned things out of my personal space.

But I didn't want to touch them again. I felt unclean, knowing I'd already handled most of those pictures. Standing, I washed my hands—three times—before brushing my teeth to get the taste of vomit out of my mouth. Still shaking, I walked into the bedroom, but I kept my distance from the scattered photos as I sprinted to the kitchen.

After finding a trash bag and some tongs, I went back to my room and put everything into the bag.

But as I was about to carry them out to the garbage chute, I realized I couldn't just toss them. I needed to tell the authorities about this. Shit, how did I even do that? I couldn't just call 9-1-1 and tell them I thought some guy was possibly stalking me. The dispatcher would probably laugh her head off at me.

Sighing, I picked up my phone and called my agent. Cathryn Schneider had been in the business for decades; she must have dealt with similar shit before. She would know what I needed to do.

"Hey, doll!" Cathryn greeted after the fourth ring. "Listen, how do you feel about doing a musical? I just had a script land on my desk, and I think you would be perfect for it. Your father has the voice of a fucking god, so I know you must have at least a little musical talent."

"Um, I can sing," I assured her, but my voice shook with a mixture of fear and anxiety. I quickly cleared it, hating that I sounded so weak. "That isn't why I'm calling, C."

"Uh oh," she said. "This doesn't sound good."

I quickly told her what happened and heard her grumble something I didn't catch.

"Fucking pervs," she seethed. "Okay, I'm on my way to your place right now. I'll turn the bag and everything in it over to the authorities. My PR people will make sure this doesn't leak to the press. Your dad will have a coronary if he hears about this."

I gulped. The thought of what this might do to my dad hadn't even entered my head. But now that she'd put that image in my brain, I suddenly couldn't stop shaking. "No!" I cried. "You can't let that happen, Cathryn!"

Nearly losing my dad to liver disease, then Pop-Pop dying so suddenly, made the idea of something taking my dad from me more terrifying than the creep who'd sent those pictures.

"I won't," she rushed to assure me. "This is just between you and me right now. When I talk to the cops about this, I'll make sure they keep your information confidential."

At her reassurance, I began to relax a little. "I-I think I'm going to go to a hotel for a few days," I told her. "I just feel too exposed here right now."

I could have gone to my parents' house, or even to Palmer's apartment, but that would mean having to explain why I didn't want to stay at my own place. Palmer would get hysterical, but my parents would go ballistic, and I didn't want to stress any of them out with this shit. Mom had been kind of lost since Pop-Pop's passing, and I couldn't function thinking about how much pressure this would put on my dad.

"Understandable, doll. You pack yourself a bag and be ready by the time I get there. I'll have my driver drop you off at whatever hotel you prefer. Just in case this bastard is following you. This way, he can't track you through your car."

Following me?

Track me?

Feeling sick all over again, I agreed then ended the call. I threw up again before I was able to pack the bag, but by the time Cathryn arrived, I was ready to go.

An hour later, as I dropped my exhausted body down onto the end of the bed in a suite in the Waldorf, I had the crazy urge to call Jordan. The events of the evening were pressing down on me, and I wanted to talk to someone I felt safe with. My first choice would be Daddy, but if I heard his voice right then, I knew I would start crying.

Then I remembered Jordan was in Milan and the huge time difference. Closing my eyes, I grabbed the extra pillow and pulled it close to my chest.

It was okay. I was a big girl. I didn't need Jordan or anyone else to hold my hand.

This was just a one-off thing. In a few days, I wouldn't even remember this guy and those stupid pictures...

I hoped.

TWO

ARELLA

Two days before Christmas Eve, the second package showed up at work. I took one look at the box, and I felt my gut twist as bile threatened to choke me. I left it in my dressing room and called Cathryn, leaving her to deal with it as I wrapped up the last scene before the holiday break that would last until February.

Cathryn arrived and promised to turn over the box to the appropriate authorities, but all I could do was nod. I didn't even want to know what was in the box, too sickened by the memories of the contents of the last one. But this wasn't unusual. There were people who'd sent me disturbing things in the past.

Just not to this extent.

I didn't want anything to do with it. Getting emotional in any way over this kind of shit was just what people like this wanted. To get in my head, scare me, throw me off my game. Well, it wasn't going to work.

Even if I was scared and sickened by those first pictures, I wasn't going to let it bother me.

At least, not on the surface.

The fact that I was cowering mentally was something this sonofabitch would never know about.

I went back to my hotel and showered, but by the time I was done, I still felt unclean and stayed under the spray until I couldn't take the heat any longer. Determined to put the whole thing out of my mind, I finished wrapping the last of the presents I'd recently bought for my sisters and prepared for Aunt Emmie's party.

Arriving late to the big event, I was just in time to see Shaw and Piper helping a bleeding and groaning Cannon into the back of Jagger's car. I waved at them, but I didn't stop to ask questions as I sprinted toward my aunt's house.

I pressed the doorbell but didn't bother to wait for someone to answer. The dim roar of voices made me smile as I walked into the living room. My gaze shifted quickly around the room until I spotted my parents. Mom was talking with Uncle Linc and Aunt Dallas, while Daddy was off to himself, rocking my nephew in his arms.

The biggest grin was on Daddy's face as he stared down at his grandson, talking softly to him. My heart melted at how happy he looked, and I could have sworn I heard Conrad cooing back at him in response.

"Arella." I turned at the sound of my name and smiled when I saw Lyric and his wife, Mila. The beautiful brunette looked like she was about to pop at any minute, her stomach stretched to the point of agony by the twin boys she was pregnant with. But she didn't look the least bit miserable to me.

If anything, she looked like she could have gladly fit another beast-sized baby in there and been all too happy with the discomfort. It was kind of unfair that she was so gorgeous, as huge as her belly was right then. I felt a small pang of envy but didn't know why.

Maybe it had something to do with the way my cousin was looking at her like she was his entire world. That was what I'd wanted on my eighteenth birthday...

Pushing those thoughts aside, I hugged Lyric, then kissed Mila's cheek. "Okay, sexy. I'm seriously pissed that you look this good while waddling," I teased and laughed when she snorted.

"Shaw told me it's the new strut for the catwalk," she snickered. "Everyone will be waddling in bikinis this time next year."

"Speaking of Shaw, I just saw her and Piper putting Cannon in the back of Jags's car. What's up with that?"

Lyric pressed his lips together in a tight line before blowing out a harsh sigh. "So, you didn't see Luca?"

I gasped and quickly glanced around for Violet, hoping she didn't overhear us as I shook my head. "No. He's here?" I finally spotted my blond cousin standing with her husband, talking to Mia. She looked radiant as she smiled up at Remington with her heart in her eyes while he rubbed his hand over her growing baby bump.

"Relax, Arella. Vi set it up for him to be here." I felt my jaw drop, sure he was joking. "She had Aunt Emmie set it up," he amended.

"Oh, okay. That makes so much more sense." Kind of. "But why?"

"To get my parents and hers to make up," he said with a shrug. "It worked. But I had some serious doubts when Vi and Remington first showed up."

"And then Baby Cage made an appearance. For about two seconds," Mila said in a quiet voice. "And Luca chased him out the door. I'm guessing he caused some real damage?"

Remembering how badly Cannon was moaning and

groaning, I grinned wickedly. "From the sound of it, I'd say possible internal damage. It's nothing he doesn't deserve, though."

I spoke to the couple for a few more minutes before my dad finally spotted me. I saw his blue-gray eyes light up, and something inside me warmed like it always did. There were daddy's girls, and there were Drake Stevenson's girls. My sisters and I knew just how lucky we were to have him as our father, and we never forgot that for even a second. Excusing myself when he called my name, I made my way through the crowd and hugged my favorite man in the universe.

When Daddy wrapped an arm around me, all the stress of the past few days started to melt away. I pressed my face into his shoulder and inhaled slowly, needing the safety of my father's arms to calm my racing heart and mind.

But then Conrad gave a gurgle and tugged on my hair. He was so tiny, barely able to hold his head up on his own yet, but he was the most beautiful little baby boy I'd ever set eyes on. I couldn't tell yet if he looked more like Nevaeh or Braxton, but one thing for sure was that he'd inherited those alluring Stevenson eyes.

Laughing, I blew a raspberry at my adorable nephew and kissed his chubby cheek, earning me a drooly, toothless grin. "Hey there, little man." I rubbed my nose against his, making him giggle. According to my older sister, he hadn't stopped laughing since he'd first started only the week before, and I had to admit, it was the most precious sound I'd ever heard. "How's Auntie's favorite little man?"

Daddy adjusted him in his arms. "He's wet, actually. I'm going to hand him over to one of his parents." He grinned. "One of the perks of being the G-Pop."

I rolled my eyes at the name he'd come up for himself for his grandson. "I'm still not feeling that title, Daddy."

He gave me a pout. "But I thought about it long and hard, Arie. Your mom likes it."

"What does Mom like?" she asked as she came up beside us.

"Conrad calling Daddy 'G-Pop,'" I supplied, and she quickly schooled her face, even though I saw the flicker of humor in her eyes. After how sad she'd been since Pop-Pop died, I was relieved to see even that small flash of happiness from her.

"Of course I do," she was quick to reassure.

Daddy grunted. "I don't care if you two like it or not. I'm sticking with G-Pop."

"But what if Conrad doesn't call you 'G-Pop'?" I asked, and Mom and I shared a conspiratorial look before Daddy could catch on. We could so easily teach Conrad to say something else that was less cheesy.

"Then I'll have to accept that," he said with reluctance. "But I'm going to try my best to get him to use it. I don't want the same grandpa title as everyone else."

"What's wrong with 'Grandpa'? I like it—a lot, actually."

He shook his head. "Boring. I'm Drake Stevenson. I need a cool title, kid."

I had a feeling Mom and I were going to lose this battle, but I didn't mind if we did. If it made him happy, I wasn't going to take it away from him. He deserved every drop of happiness the world had to offer.

"He's looking a little full in the tushy," Mom commented as she took Conrad. The baby giggled when she kissed his cheeks. "Come on, you rotten little devil. G-Mom will get you a dry diaper."

I groaned.

"What?" she asked, then winked. "If you can't change it, embrace it."

Daddy followed her out of the living room with his hand on her ass. I wanted to gag at the proof that my parents were still very much sexually active, but part of me thought it was romantic and so damn adorable, it made my heart squeeze.

For the next hour, I made a point to talk to everyone. I loved each person in this house—some more than others, but I loved them, nonetheless. Eventually, I journeyed into the kitchen where a buffet-style meal was set up. For the moment, there was no one else in there to judge me, so I grabbed one of the plates, tore open a huge yeast roll and smothered it with mashed potatoes, ham, green bean casserole, and a huge scoop of mac and cheese.

It was while my mouth was full of my first bite that Jordan walked into the kitchen. Mentally groaning, I grabbed a napkin and wiped my mouth as I quickly chewed and swallowed while he walked toward me. From the set of his shoulders and the look on his too-sexy face, I got the weird feeling he was determined about something, but I didn't understand what it could be.

"What are you doing, hiding in here?" he asked with a small grin teasing at his lips.

"Feeding my face, actually," I told him with a shrug. "My stomach started making angry noises, so I figured I needed to feed the beast." Wiping my mouth again, I tilted my head at him. "You're awfully late to the party this year. Normally, you're one of the first to arrive, usually right behind Mia."

"I stopped by your apartment, thinking we would ride together, but I stood outside your door for a good ten minutes before your neighbor told me she hadn't seen you in at least a week." His jaw clenched as if that angered him, and I nearly rolled my eyes.

"You didn't think to maybe call and ask if I wanted to ride with you?" I dropped my plate on the counter beside the sink and grabbed a soft drink from one of the ice chests set out for the guests. There was everything anyone could possibly want, except alcohol. Out of respect for my dad's sobriety, Aunt Emmie never served booze at any of her parties.

As I uncapped the diet cola, I saw him rub a hand over the back of his neck. "I wanted to surprise you. I didn't even get back to town until this evening, and I went to your place straight from the airport. Work has been kicking my ass lately."

Yeah, I thought. *Work, sure. It couldn't have possibly been Letizia or the Danish princess or any number of other redheads who warmed your bed.*

Reminding myself it was none of my business and that I'd moved on from this guy and the future I'd envisioned us having, I decided to skip the main course and eat dessert. Turning away from him, I grabbed a new plate and dished up a huge slice of chocolate cake.

Not caring if he saw me stuffing my face, I picked up a fork and crammed a huge bite into my mouth.

"Damn, that looks good," he said with a groan. When he picked up a fork for himself, I thought he was going to get his own, but instead, he stuck it in mine.

"Hey," I whined when he lifted a bite of my cake to his mouth. "That's mine."

His grin was wicked and made my heart do a crazy little flip, while lower, I had a different kind of uncomfortable going on. Without thinking, I pressed my thighs together to try to relieve the sudden ache and watched as his eyes darkened.

"And it's fucking delicious," he growled as he started to lower his head. "But I need another taste."

I held my breath, wondering if he was going to kiss me—secretly hoping he would.

Then the kitchen door opened, and Mia walked in. "Jordan!" she squealed, and Jordan's head snapped up so fast, you would have thought he'd been caught murdering someone. "I thought I saw you come in a little while ago."

My heart sank, and I became pissed at myself for daring to hope for something I knew was never going to happen. I dropped my cake in the trash and muttered an "Excuse me" as I left the kitchen.

It suddenly felt way too hot in the house. Needing some fresh air, I kept my head down as I made my way to the front door so no one would try to speak to me. When I was out on the porch, the urge to cry faded, and it was only then that I realized I'd been fighting it.

"Stupid, stupid, stupid," I chastised myself as I stomped off the porch.

"That's not a nice thing to say about my favorite cousin," a deep voice said to my left.

I swallowed the scream that had bubbled up and then threw myself into Luca's arms when I saw him standing there with Violet's bodyguard, Jenner. The brief shot of fear straight on the heels of what had happened in the kitchen made me tremble, but that quickly passed as Luca hugged me back.

"Hey, hey," he murmured, leaning back to look down at me. He was huge, just as tall as the bodyguard and with at least ten more pounds of muscle on him. "What's wrong?"

I forced a grin and shook my head. "Nothing. Everything. A million things I can't control." I breathed in deeply, taking the chilly December air into my lungs, and lifted a shoulder. "You know how it is."

"Yeah," he agreed, keeping one arm around my shoulders. "I know exactly how it is."

I glanced between Luca and Jenner. There wasn't a strained tension between them like I would have expected. If anything, they appeared to be friendly. That just seemed weird as hell to me. Jenner, Violet's personal muscle paid for by her billionaire husband, being friends with her ex? I just couldn't wrap my head around that, but I didn't question either of them about it.

"I think I'm going to head home," I said as I pulled away from Luca, suddenly feeling so tired, I didn't think I could keep my eyes open for much longer. How I was going to drive all the way back to my hotel, I wasn't sure, but I'd figure it out. Even if I had to stop for a nap.

"Don't rush off," Luca stopped me. His gaze went to the house, and I felt him begin to tense. "I don't know if I can go back in there, Arella. I was going to go to my parents' house and just crash in my room. Could you...keep me company?"

Seeing the loneliness in his brown eyes, I didn't even hesitate. "Sure. Let's raid the pantry and eat all of Aunt Layla's junk food like we used to do when we were kids."

"Perfect." He glanced at Jenner. "Thanks for the talk, man. I'll be seeing you."

Jenner inclined his head. "Possibly sooner than either of us realizes, Mr. Thornton."

Luca stiffened. "For her sake, I really hope not."

"What was that about?" I asked once we were out of earshot of the bodyguard.

"Nothing," he deflected. "What were you running from back there?"

"Nothing."

Our gazes locked, and we both snickered. "For an award-winning actress, you can't lie for shit."

"I wasn't really trying," I excused as he unlocked the front door. We walked through the house and straight into the kitchen. He opened the pantry door and grabbed a package of Oreos and some cake icing. When I saw it, I shook my head, not wanting to think about the chocolate cake I'd abandoned to get away from Jordan and seeing him fawn all over Mia.

It was stupid. I loved Mia so damn much, but she was the one person in the world I was the most jealous of.

Luca replaced the icing and grabbed an unopened bag of Cheetos. I pushed him out of my way and started grabbing a few things, but since none of her children lived at home any longer, it seemed that Aunt Layla didn't keep very much junk food in stock.

"This is a sad stash," I grumbled as we walked up the stairs to Luca's old room.

"It really is," he agreed. "But it's better than having to go back to Aunt Emmie's and watching Violet be happy with someone else." Jaw clenched, he dropped down on the floor beside the bed and leaned his back against it. "She glows, Arella. Fucking glows."

I grasped his arm and gave it a sympathetic squeeze. "I'm sorry."

He closed his eyes. "Don't be. I'm the one who fucked everything up. I don't deserve her."

"I don't know what to say here, Luca," I told him honestly. "I want to tell you it will get better. That you'll find someone else and be happy. But I can't picture you with anyone but Vi."

"Me either." Opening his eyes, he grabbed the first

thing his fingers touched and opened the cookies. Stuffing four into his mouth, he picked up the remote to the television mounted on the wall and clicked it on. "Thanks for coming with me," he said after we'd both been silent for several long minutes. "Even if we don't do anything but sit here, it's nice to have someone to be quiet with."

I leaned my head against his arm, comforting him and accepting comfort in return. He didn't know what was going on with me, but that didn't matter. Just being beside him made things...not better, but more bearable. "Yeah, this is kind of nice."

After a while, he told me about the house he was about to close on. It was right next door to Uncle Wroth's farm and just a few miles from Uncle Axton's house. It was less than an hour's drive to work for him, but I knew he'd bought it because Violet had always loved West Bridge, Tennessee, so much.

It only made me sad for him, but I let him tell me every last detail about the place. He needed someone to just listen, and I needed someone to just sit beside and not have to worry about what was going on with my stalker or how much it had hurt that Jordan had jerked away from me earlier like I had something contagious he didn't want to catch.

Would I ever learn not to get my hopes up where Jordan Moreitti was concerned?

THREE

JORDAN

Mia waited until the door closed behind Arella before putting her hands on her hips and glaring at me. "For such a smart guy, you're pretty fucking stupid at times. You realize that, right?"

"No one told you to follow me in here," I grumbled. "Everything was going perfectly until you showed up."

She rolled her pretty green eyes at me. "Well, excuse me. I'm a little absent-minded right now. I didn't realize I was going to walk in on you about to kiss the girl." She poked me in the chest, hard. "But you didn't have to act like you got caught red-handed with the crown jewels. You just broke her heart. Again, I might add."

I scrubbed my hands over my face, knowing I'd fucked up—again—but not knowing how to fix anything. Where Arella was concerned, I didn't seem to have any game at all. It wasn't until Cole Steel died that I realized I'd fucked up in the first place. After my girl had left me standing in her kitchen after her grandfather's funeral, Mia had clued me in to how let down Arella had been that I hadn't shown up for her eighteenth birthday party.

While I'd been running to protect myself, she'd been waiting for me to make all her dreams come true. My selfishness had ruined everything, and she'd been more or less running from me ever since. The few times I'd been home since the funeral, she'd gone to dinner and the occasional movie with me, but it was obvious to me she'd put up walls that a wrecking ball would have trouble knocking down.

"What should I do?" I demanded of my best friend, pissed at her for barging in on us to begin with. I'd thought it was one of her parents interrupting, and after how cold Lana and Drake had been with me, I didn't want either of them walking in on me trying to kiss their daughter until I had that girl marked as mine. Otherwise, they might try to keep her away from me, and I was barely functioning without her as it was.

"Going after her would be my first suggestion," Mia snipped.

"Shit. Right. Okay, I'll find her." I started to head for the door, but Mia began to sway. Grasping her by the hips, I steadied her and realized she was sweating. "Holy shit, Mia. Are you sick?"

She was already fair-skinned, but she looked almost deathly pale. "Fuck, this isn't like the last time. I think I would take the nonstop morning sickness over this crap."

My eyes widened. "You're pregnant?"

She groaned. "Yes. I've been holding off on telling anyone because I want to tell Barrick as a kind of Christmas present in the morning. But I've been so dizzy that my brother has already guessed, and now you." Tears glittered in her eyes. "I wanted Barrick to be the first to know, and now I've ruined everything."

Movement at the door pulled my gaze, and I saw Barrick step silently into the room. He lifted his finger to his lips, and I shifted my attention back to Mia before she realized we weren't alone. "Why is everything ruined?" I asked her softly.

"Because he was supposed to know before anyone else. Not Jagger or you or even my parents. Just Barrick." Her chin trembled, and I tightened my hold on her. I never could stand the sight of her tears. They gutted me and made me want to eviscerate whatever had dared to cause her to cry.

I cared about Mia like no one else in my life, and even though we'd taken things too far once and only once, I'd never loved her as more than a friend. She was like family to me, and I couldn't imagine my life without her.

But what I felt for Arella? That was on a level I'd never experienced before, and I'd been screwing up left and right with her.

Other than at her grandfather's funeral and when her dad had his liver transplant surgery, I'd never really seen Arella cry, but both times had been enough to bring me to my knees.

"I've been saving this news just for Christmas because we've been trying for so long for another baby with no results, and...and...I only wanted to make it special." Her sobs hurt my heart, but it was nothing to the agonized groan Barrick released behind her.

Startled by the sound, she turned around. "Barrick," she whispered. "It...It was supposed to be..."

He enfolded her in his arms, tears already spilling down his face and into his beard. "It's the best surprise ever, firecracker," he choked out. "Adding another baby to our family is the best present you could ever give me, second only to you loving me."

Giving them a moment to themselves, I silently left

them in the kitchen and went in search of Arella. It took me twenty minutes to check the entire house before I asked one of her many cousins if they had seen her.

"I think I saw her leave," Remington Sawyer informed me as he and Violet stood in a group with Violet's parents and a few others. "That was a while ago, though."

I muttered a thanks and quickly made my way out of the house. Her leaving could be a good thing, I told myself. We would be alone, and I could finally tell her everything I should have already said.

But when I got outside, I saw her car was still there. "Fuck," I groaned. "Where did you go?"

"Something wrong?"

I turned at the deep voice I didn't recognize and found some hulking goon in a suit. Figuring he was one of Barrick's men, I stepped toward him. "Arella Stevenson. You know her?"

He tilted his head to the left. "She went with her cousin to the Thorntons'."

"Lyric?" Luca hadn't been home for Christmas in a few years, from what I understood.

"No, sir. It was Luca." He opened a car door and got behind the wheel. "I guess they're doing some family bonding. Hadn't seen each other in a while, from what I heard."

"Thanks," I told him, but I just stood there, trying to decide what course of action I should take. Go to the Thorntons' and carry her out? Wait for her? Go to her place and ambush her there when she got home?

"You look like a stalker standing out here glaring at nothing," a soft voice said behind me.

Sighing, I turned my head to find Aunt Gabs standing on the sidewalk beside me. I hadn't even heard her approach. "Don't be surprised if I suddenly turn into one," I grumbled before bending my head to kiss her cheek.

"Girl trouble?" she asked with amusement lighting her brown eyes. My only response was to grunt, causing her to laugh. "That's the response I get whenever Asher has the same problem."

"Yeah? And what advice do you give him when he has these problems?"

My rocker aunt lifted her brows in surprise. "If you need my advice, sweetheart, all you have to do is ask."

"Aunt Gabs," I groaned. "Just tell me what I should do to make my girl—"

She gasped. "*Your girl?* You're claiming this one?" She gave a happy little dance. "Does LeeLee know?"

"Mom doesn't know. Yet." No one but Mia knew the truth, and I wanted to fix that. Arella needed to know I wanted more than just her friendship before I told my parents...or hers. "As soon as I get this girl locked down, I'll tell Mom. I promise. Until then, maybe you can suggest how I could go about doing just that."

"What, locking her down?" I shrugged in answer, and she sighed dramatically. "If this girl is who I'm thinking it is, you aren't just going to 'lock her down,' as you so crassly put it. The way you appear in all those stupid tabloids, I honestly thought you were smarter and smoother than this Jordan."

"You know none of that filth is true," I scoffed. "I can't even stand those girls."

"Yet you're in so, so many pictures in nightclubs, or coming out of nightclubs, with them. Usually with their lipstick on some part of your face or clothing."

Clenching my jaw, I didn't try to defend myself. We

both knew the truth, and I wasn't about to discuss pointless shit with her.

"Okay, fine. So you want to show this girl you're serious about her?" I nodded, and she smiled sweetly. "Then you need to come home and stay home. Be there for her, show her that you want her and only her. No more pictures of slutty redheads hanging all over you."

I started to argue about the redheads, but she lifted both hands. "Yeah, yeah. I know your dumbass father has you wining and dining these girls to get their daddies' business, but you're going to have to choose who is more of a priority. The idiot who nearly lost the love of his life because he was without a doubt the dumbest motherfucker I'd ever met. Or the girl who could have her choice of any guy she wants and keeps running from you because she thinks you're secretly in love with your best friend?"

Shock hit me, knocking the air out of my chest, causing me to wheeze when I whispered, "She thinks that?"

"Of course she thinks that!" Throwing up her hands, she glared at me. "I love you like you are my own, Jordan, but I swear you're just as stupid as your father sometimes."

Gritting my teeth, I ignored her continued verbal abuse of my dad. He wasn't as stupid as she let on, just had made repeatedly stupid decisions where my mom was concerned all those years ago. But she was completely right. Apparently, I was just as bad as my father if I couldn't stop fucking up with my girl.

How the fuck could she possibly think I was in love with Mia? *Why* would she even think that? I admit, fucking her was a mistake; I never should have done that. But she'd been hurting, devastated after finding out the future she'd always envisioned for herself was over. She'd needed someone to make her forget her broken heart for a little while. Honestly, it had been weird for me. Afterward, I'd felt sick to my stomach.

Mia was hot, smoking hot, but I didn't love her like that. She might have gotten my dick hard, but a guy either would have to be related to her, gay, or dead not to get hard at the sight of her. Still, it had felt wrong, and I'd never regretted anything so much in my life.

Until now.

Now, I regretted every move I hadn't made to make Arella mine.

FOUR
ARELLA

I woke with a start when I heard a giggle. My eyes snapped open, and it took me a moment to realize where I was. Beside me, Luca was softly snoring, a pillow under his head, while his huge body was stretched out on the floor. The television was still on, but the backlight was down low and the volume was muted. I wasn't sure if Luca had pulled the comforter down over the both of us or if maybe one of his parents had.

The giggle came again, and then I heard Uncle Jesse's deep chuckle. They were right outside the door and, by the sounds I was hearing, about to get hot and heavy. I cringed, not wanting to hear them going at it, and quickly reached for my phone.

Turning my head, I found it on the floor beside me and glanced at the time. It was a little after one in the morning, and I figured my aunt and uncle were just now getting home from Aunt Emmie's party. I'd been asleep for at least two hours.

Sitting up, I pushed my hair out of my face and rose to my feet. By the time I got to the door and chanced sticking my head out, the master bedroom door was just closing. Breathing a sigh of relief that I wasn't going to catch my uncle stripping my aunt in the hall, I quietly left the house.

Outside, I noticed that most of the vehicles were gone, and I rushed toward my car. But I'd barely gone a few yards when I remembered the stalker. What if he was watching me?

"Stupid," I muttered to myself. It was the middle of the night, and no one was around that I could see. What if the stalker tried to snatch me?

My sprint turned into a full-on run, but when I got to my car, I realized my purse—and more importantly, my keys—was still in Aunt Emmie's house. Groaning, I glanced at her front door, wondering if she was still awake.

"I got your purse earlier."

A small yelp left me at the sound of an unexpected voice. Jerking around, I found Jordan had unfolded himself from the driver's seat of my car and was standing there watching me intently. He held up my purse, and I could only assume my keys were in there.

Pressing a hand to my still-pounding heart, I glared at him. "What are you doing here?"

His jaw clenched so hard, I thought it might shatter if he gritted his teeth. "I was waiting for you so we could talk."

A gust of wind blew, making me regret not having brought a jacket. Wrapping my arms around myself to fight off the chill, I ignored the heat pooling low in my tummy at the way his dark eyes were trailing over me. I hadn't stopped to glance at myself in a mirror, so I had no clue what I might look like, but I'd bet my hair was a tangled mess and my makeup was probably smeared under my eyes.

The way Jordan was hungrily eating up the sight of me, however, told me he liked what he was seeing.

Need made my inner muscles clench hard, but I knew better than to think he would even make a move. And if he did, was it because he wanted *me*, or because he couldn't have the girl he really wanted?

"It's late, Jordan. I'm not in the mood to talk." I walked around the car, expecting him to step back so I could get behind the wheel.

His arms wrapped around me so fast it was like a cobra striking, making me gasp. One second, I was a foot away; the next, my front was plastered against the front of his body while he pressed me back against my car. Liquid desire was already soaking my panties and smearing on my inner thighs. The cool night air flowing up my dress made me shiver.

Jordan pressed his forehead to mine and inhaled deeply. "Let me clear something up here and now," he growled. The sound was sexy as hell, vibrating out of him and making my nipples pebble into painful little points against my bra. "Mia is my best friend. I love her."

Pain ricocheted inside me, and it took a strength I didn't know I possessed to hold back the whimper aching to be released.

"But I swear, I'm not *in love* with her."

I pulled my head back as far as I could and blinked up at him. "Why are you telling me?"

"Because someone brought it to my attention tonight that you were under a huge misconception." He pushed a few locks of my tangled hair behind my ear before trailing his fingers down my neck. I held back the whine at how good his touch felt, but I couldn't stop the goose bumps that popped up in his wake. "I should have cleared this up years ago. But I didn't realize you thought my heart was engaged in that way with Mia."

"You slept with her," I reminded him. "And every girl you go out with looks like her in some shape or form."

"Sleeping with her was the biggest mistake of my life. I regretted it the second it happened. If I could go back and change it, I would. But I can't, baby." His exploring fingers trailed down my bare arm before entwining with mine and holding my hand prisoner. "And you should know more than anyone that just because I'm in trash mags with someone doesn't mean I'm sleeping with them."

Angrily, I tilted my chin up. "Maybe you should tell that to Letizia."

His laugh was so deep, it made his entire body shake with it, causing my own to clench as my clit pulsed. I loved the sound of his laugh. It never failed to cause happiness to explode inside me, but right then, I wanted to punch him in the face.

"Baby, Letizia is delusional. The only reason I see her so often is because of work." Leaning in, he brushed his nose over mine, causing the sarcastic retort I'd been about to spew at him to dry up in my throat.

Damn, why did that feel so intimate? It was like he was nuzzling something deep in my soul. When he did it again, I couldn't contain my little mewl of contentment and melted against him ever so slightly.

Jordan groaned as the sound left me and thrust his lower body against mine. It was then that I focused on his hardness. Holy shit, he was huge. My lashes drifted closed, and I felt a little faint as he twitched against me. It was like he had a third leg in his pants, for fuck's sake.

"Um, Jordan, how..." I paused and licked my suddenly parched lips. "How do you even walk around in this condition without ripping your pants?"

When he didn't answer, I lifted my lashes and found his

gaze locked on to my mouth. Nervously, I licked my lips again and was fascinated by how his eyes dilated. My breathing started to pick up, my chest lifting and falling, making my tits jiggle slightly in the confines of my bra. The dress I was wearing was low-cut, so I knew it was giving him a nice little peep show of my cleavage.

Still holding my hand in one of his, he lifted the other. Skimming his middle finger over the collar of my top, he brushed his nose against mine once again. "I have to go back to Italy."

Disappointment made my eyes sting with tears, and I clenched them closed.

"But I swear, as soon as I get back, things are going to be different, baby. Once I'm home, I'm not leaving without you again." He cupped my breast through my dress and bra, squeezing as if he were trying to mark me. "Just give me a little more time."

Swallowing the lump threatening to choke me, I put my free hand against his chest and pushed firmly. "I gave up on you a long time ago, Jordan," I told him honestly, meeting his gaze. "You're free to do whatever you want. There's no need to make me promises or ask me for them in return."

"Maybe not," he murmured, pulling me close once again. "But I'm making them anyway. When I get home, I'm staking my claim, Arella."

"Just because you call something yours doesn't mean it's true." I tried to push him back again, but he wouldn't budge. "Jordan, let me go."

"Never," he breathed against my lips before he sealed his mouth to mine.

My brain told me to fight him, to push him away and kick him in the balls. Who knew where that mouth of his had been recently?

But my heart gave a happy little scream, and I melted against him, kissing him back hungrily. His hands cupped my ass, lifting me up. My fingers thrust into his hair, while my legs automatically went around his waist, causing my dress to hike up until his cock was pressed right against my soaked core.

"Fuck yeah, baby," he groaned as I cried out into his mouth when he rubbed against my clit. "That sound is the sexiest thing I have ever heard. As soon as I get back, I'm going to find out exactly what you sound like when I make you come all over my cock."

The only response I could muster was a weak little whimper as I rubbed myself against his hardness.

"Really not the sight I was expecting—or even wanting—to see tonight."

My head snapped up at the sound of Lyric's voice. I glanced around and saw him and Mila standing on the sidewalk. Mila had a tired but amused smile on her face, but my cousin was looking at us with a disgusted frown.

Still breathing hard from our kiss, Jordan shot him a glare. "No one told you to look, Thornton."

Lyric snorted. "Kinda hard not to see you two going at it like that, man. Maybe you should take this somewhere else before one of the parentals sees you two."

My body felt like it was on fire, but reality was setting in and making me cool off way too quick. I started to shiver, and Jordan set me on my feet. "I-I should go," I stuttered.

"Night, Arella," Mila called, tugging her husband toward his parents' house.

"N-night," I muttered, moving to get into my car.

Once I was seated, Jordan crouched down beside me and cupped my face. "I don't know how long I'll be gone this time, but I swear it is going to be the last time unless you go with me."

"Jordan—"

"I'll call you tomorrow," he cut me off. Leaning in, he brushed a kiss on my cheek, and I had to clench my hands around the steering wheel to keep from pulling him in for another deep kiss. "Merry Christmas, baby."

FIVE
ARELLA

SINCE MY LITTLE BROTHER DIDN'T BELIEVE IN SANTA any longer, we didn't have to wake up ridiculously early to open presents at my parents' house, so I didn't arrive at their house until lunchtime the next day. I was just in time to help Mom make a huge brunch for everyone before we gathered in the living room to exchange gifts.

Ever since Daddy had spent one Christmas in the hospital recovering from his liver transplant, I hadn't taken spending this particular holiday with my family for granted. I wanted to make the most of every minute I had with any of them, and I wasn't going to waste a single second.

Pushing all thoughts of Jordan and the stalker out of my mind, I enjoyed the day with my siblings, brother-in-law, and parents. Cuddling with Conrad was the best part, though, and I fell asleep on the couch with him on my chest. The sweet baby scent filled my nose, and his slight weight and the utter trust he had in me to love and protect him had my eyes drifting shut to the sight of his precious face.

"Arie." My dad's voice roused me from my restful sleep

as he lifted my nephew off my chest. "Time for dinner, sweetheart."

Other than the nap I'd taken the night before with Luca, this was the most I'd actually slept since I'd gotten the first package from the stalker. I couldn't close my eyes for longer than an hour or two at a time because I was always scared someone was watching me. Even in my hotel room, I couldn't get comfortable, thinking the stalker could possibly find me at any moment.

I could have told Nevaeh and Braxton and gotten a bodyguard within minutes, but I knew my sister would tell one or both of our parents, and I just couldn't stomach the thought of either of them stressing over me. I wouldn't be responsible for my dad worrying himself sick, and Mom was just starting to get back to herself after losing Pop-Pop.

Besides, I was an adult. I could deal with all of this on my own. And it was just two little packages. It wasn't as if this idiot was actually trying to get close to me.

At least, that was what I kept telling myself. I'd repeated it over and over again since the first package, but I wasn't so sure I believed it.

After dinner, my parents talked me into spending the night in my old room, but Nevaeh and her little family went to their own house, which was just down the block. Really, Mom didn't have to try very hard to get me to agree. My parents lived in a gated community. The guards worked tirelessly to keep unwanted people out.

Which was why when I walked to my car late the next morning and found a box sitting in my passenger seat, my knees went weak.

Shaking, I got behind the wheel and fought my gag reflex as I called Cathryn on my drive out of the neighborhood.

"Bring it to me, doll," she said grimly. "And I'm going to suggest you get out of town for a bit. Somewhere this person can't easily find you. After seeing the contents of the last box, I was worried, but you didn't want to know what was in it."

I breathed in deeply, trying to keep the panic from swallowing me whole. "I still don't, but I think you should tell me."

"There were pictures, just like last time. On one of the pictures, he left a message and called you 'little bird' again. At the bottom of the box, there was a dead bird, Arella. The detective I've been working with on this to keep it under the radar said it looked like the poor thing's neck was broken."

My gaze jerked to the box on my seat, scared at what could possibly be in there. Was it another dead bird? Ah fuck, I hoped not.

Tears filled my eyes, and I had to blink them away quickly so I could see to drive. "I-I got an offer to go stay with one of my cousins," I told her in a choked voice.

"I'll make the arrangements," she offered. "We'll book you a flight under one of the aliases that we use when you have to do press tours."

"I'm on my way to your office now."

"Listen, doll. I know we both agreed your parents shouldn't find out about this, but if this guy was at their house..."

One of my tears spilled over my cheek. "As long as I'm not around, he won't bother them." Which meant I had to stay away from the two people I loved the most to protect them. Fuck, this wasn't going to be easy.

"You need private security."

"I know," I whispered. "But not yet. Give me a little time, Cathryn. I have a few things I need to figure out. No one will bother me where I'm going. I don't even think anyone knows Luca moved."

"All right. Maybe we'll get lucky and this bastard will just give up if you stay in hiding long enough."

"Yeah," I muttered. "Maybe."

But in my gut, I knew this guy wasn't just going to slither back into the dark, disgusting hole he crawled out of.

--

I called Luca to let him know I was taking him up on his offer to help him decorate his new house. But he reminded me that he hadn't closed yet and wouldn't until after the new year. He was still at his parents' house for a few more days, but he told me I could fly back with him if I wanted.

The problem with that was he would draw too much attention on his own. If I were with him, it would stir up the paps even more, and then whoever this stalker was would know exactly where I was. Telling Luca I'd let him know, I drove to Cathryn's to drop off the box.

Detective Kirtner was standing in her office when I walked in. He was a middle-aged man with a bald patch on top of his head. Skinny, he was dressed in a cheap suit. His face was set in grave lines as he looked at the box I was carrying. I couldn't bring myself to touch the damn thing with my bare hands, so I'd found a towel in my trunk from one of my trips to the gym and used it to hold the box.

He instructed me to put it on Cathryn's desk and then pulled on a pair of gloves.

"I don't know if I want to see what's in there," I told him as I backed away.

He turned and gave me a hard look. "Miss Stevenson, you're going to have to stop running from reality here. This is serious, and you need to be aware of just how far this person is willing to go to get your attention."

"He's right, doll," Cathryn told me with a twist of her mouth. "You need to see how dangerous this is."

I steeled my spine and nodded, but I kept a few feet between the desk and me.

Cathryn stood beside the detective as he used a pocketknife to tear through the tape on the box and then opened the flaps. The first thing he pulled out was a stack of glossy photos. "Same as last time," he muttered, and Cathryn nodded, watching him flip through the stack over his shoulder.

"Gross," my agent muttered, making a disgusted face at whatever she saw. "This guy is seriously perverted."

"Unfortunately, this isn't the worst I've ever seen," Kirtner informed her stoically. "But he has a real fetish for her preferred lotion, it seems."

Once he got to the last picture, he turned it over. "It says, 'Merry Christmas, little bird. Next year, we will celebrate it together.'" He nodded to Cathryn, who opened a zip-top baggie, and he placed the stack of photos inside. She sealed it up, and he took it from her before writing on it with a black Sharpie. Once that was done, he placed it on the desk and reached back into the box.

"Doll, I hope you have a strong stomach," was the only warning I got before Kirtner pulled out the poor little dead bird.

A pained cry left me when I saw the way its neck was twisted, tears blinding me so I couldn't see the pitiful creature in the detective's large hand. "It's identical to the last one," he said with a shake of his head. "Wouldn't be surprised if he keeps birds for pets."

"Is that a parakeet?" I sobbed. "It was so pretty. The colors of its wings..." I hiccuped then shuddered. "Oh God, I-I feel sick."

Thankfully, a trash can was right beside the door, and I picked it up just in time to empty my stomach contents into it. Mom had made another huge breakfast that morning, and I regretted eating so many pancakes.

When I was done, I felt cold and empty, my heart broken for the tiny, beautiful bird. Shivering, I moved to one of the chairs and dropped down onto it. As tears poured down my face, I grabbed my phone.

Without thinking, I pulled up Jordan's contact information, but my thumb hovered over his number. I couldn't call my parents about this, but there was someone I could talk to. I needed to hear his voice.

No, I moaned to myself as I held back another sob. I needed him to hold me, but he was in fucking Italy.

Christmas Eve, he'd said he would call me the next day, but he never did. I'd stayed off social media, afraid of what I would find he'd been up to when he'd made me promises.

Promises I knew deep down he wouldn't keep.

That didn't stop me from wanting him there with me in that moment. To hold me, protect me, tell me everything was going to be okay because he wouldn't let this sick fuck touch me.

"What are you doing when I need you, Jordan?" I whispered as I angrily shoved my phone back into my purse.

SIX
ARELLA

I changed hotels for a few days until Luca flew home, but by New Year's, I was sick of my own company and ready to be around people. I'd called my parents, but I'd made excuses not to go to their house or have them meet me anywhere, just in case this stalker dickhead was watching me.

The first week of January, I landed in Nashville and rented a car. My plane ticket and rental were in the name of one of my aliases, just in case someone was watching my credit card activity. It was insane to me that someone would care enough to track me down in such a way, but Cathryn and Detective Kirtner both said it was a big possibility and I had to be extra careful.

Needing to put all thoughts of the stalker out of my mind, I threw myself into decorating my cousin's new home. But it wasn't as easy as I imagined it would be. Not the decorating, that was easy, and Luca seemed to love the way I transformed his house.

No, it was trying to keep my mind off the fact that someone was obsessed with me. Calling me "little bird" and then breaking the necks of poor little innocent birds to get my attention. On top of that, Jordan still hadn't so much as tried to contact me, reinforcing my theory that when I was out of sight, I was definitely out of his mind.

The fact that he was in dozens of tabloids with Letizia was enough for me to know that he'd been full of shit Christmas Eve. I'd told myself repeatedly that I was over him, but that kiss and his promises had given me hope. I was just the stupid girl who had let her heart believe we might have something special.

By the time most of the rooms in Luca's house were complete, it was time for me to get back to work. Filming for the final episodes of my show was getting ready to commence, and I needed to return to California to finish out my contract.

There had been no more packages delivered to my apartment, something Cathryn had assured me of since Detective Kirtner was stopping by to check out my place every few days. He'd also done a few drive-bys of my parents' house, just to give me a little more peace of mind, as well as checking the studio.

I was optimistic that the stalker had given up on me and I could go back to living my life as usual. When I got back to LA, I went straight home and slept in my own bed for the first time in over six weeks. My housekeeper had still been cleaning a few days a week, so the place was spotless when I walked through the door.

Sighing contentedly, I showered and then crashed after having spent the entire day traveling. I had to be at the studio early the next morning, so even though it was barely eight in the evening, I went right to bed.

For the next two weeks, I was so busy with not only filming but doing press for the final episodes that I didn't have more than a few minutes to myself, and those were dedicated to sleep. But all the work and trying to figure out which part I wanted to take next seemed trivial when Violet's husband died.

The funeral was kept low-key so the press didn't get hold of the news that billionaire Remington Sawyer had passed in his sleep and poor Vi didn't get dragged through the mud along with it. No one had even known Remington was sick except for Vi and a few others.

Dressed in a simple black dress that fell to my knees, I arrived at the church just as everyone else was sitting down for the service. Over the past few days, I'd wanted to visit my cousin to check on her, but my parents had told me Violet wasn't in any condition to receive guests. Mom told me that Luca was with her, however. While that blew my mind, it was also a relief.

I knew Violet was in the best of hands with Luca, so I didn't worry about her falling apart like she had when she'd broken up with him.

The church was huge, but there were barely fifty people in attendance, and most of those were Violet's closest relatives. Remington hadn't had any family left, which was heartbreaking. He'd been alone most of his life. Violet had given him a family, was carrying his baby in her womb, and loved him completely. It didn't seem fair that he had been taken before he'd even gotten to hold his daughter or tell her how much he loved her.

I couldn't imagine losing my own father before I got the chance to meet and know what an amazing man he was.

Heart aching for my cousin and her unborn child, I took a seat in the back so I didn't disturb anyone.

But it seemed I wasn't the only late arrival. No sooner

was I seated than someone dropped down into the pew beside me.

His scent hit me as he shifted to unbutton his suit jacket. Forcing down the disappointment and pain his nearness brought back to the surface, I slowly turned my head and found Jordan looking down at me with veiled eyes. Damn, but I loved his eyes. Such a rich brown color that made me think of maple syrup pouring over warm pancakes. Or a pool of thick molasses so deep, I could swim in the delicious sweetness.

"Hey," he murmured softly.

"Hi," I gritted out. Folding my hands around each other, I jerked my head back around to focus on the minister. But as I did, my gaze landed on the beautiful woman sitting several pews ahead of us.

Alexis Moreitti was watching her son and me with a guarded expression, and I quickly looked away from her probing stare. I couldn't tell if she disapproved of us sitting together or if she was angry we had both arrived so late. Either way, the look in her pretty eyes made my chest ache because it only drove home for me just how much Jordan and I didn't belong together.

It was glaringly obvious to me that his mom didn't like me. It wouldn't have been the first time a guy's parents didn't think I was good enough to be with their son. There were a few guys I was only friends with, but their mothers had basically shunned me. I was too...much for some people. I'd been called a flake, an airhead, and any number of other names by overprotective mommies who thought their precious little boys were too good for the likes of me.

But I'd never wanted to be accepted so much in my life as I did by Alexis Moreitti.

I craved for her to smile at me as I'd seen her smile at

Mia so many times. As if I were one of her own, maybe even as the daughter she'd never had. I knew it was wishful thinking, but I'd lain in bed countless nights fantasizing about it. Which was ridiculous.

Just like it was ridiculous to imagine Jordan and I belonged together.

As the service continued and Violet's broken sobs tore at something deep inside me, Jordan shifted beside me. His arm went along the back of the pew, and I felt his fingers grazing over my shoulder through my dress. Once he was settled, his fingertips skimmed the bare skin of my upper arm, drawing tiny circles that left goose bumps in their wake.

I shrugged his hand away and scooted over so that he wasn't as close, but he followed until his thigh brushed against mine. As pissed and disillusioned as I was where this guy was concerned, my body couldn't help but react to his nearness. Heat pooled low in my tummy, and an ache began to throb between my legs. I was disgusted with myself for feeling even remotely attracted to the asshole, especially at a funeral.

He wrapped his fingers around my arm and pulled me in closer as he lowered his head. "Why did you block my number?" he whispered, but there was no mistaking the hurt and underlying anger in his voice.

"I didn't," I hissed, keeping my eyes trained straight ahead.

"Yes, you did. I've been calling you every damn day, Arella. Texting you practically every hour. And nothing goes through." He tightened his fingers, and he nuzzled my ear with his nose, making me shiver as his breath fanned over my neck, exposed from the way I'd styled my hair. "If this is my punishment, I surrender, baby. Just give me a chance."

Angrily, I pulled my phone from my purse and opened my contacts. Clicking on his name, I brought up his information to show him I hadn't blocked him—

Only to find that he was, in fact, blocked.

My hands turned clammy instantly, and I nearly dropped my phone as they began to shake. I hadn't blocked him, so who the fuck had?

Mind racing, my heart pounding against my rib cage with my growing fear, I tried to remember the last time I'd actually spoken to Jordan on the phone or via text, and I couldn't recall. It had been at least two weeks before Christmas, I was sure of that much.

The only time my phone was ever out of my sight was at work. I usually kept it in my dressing room with the rest of my things so it didn't distract me while I was filming.

Had...?

I began to tremble.

Had the stalker been in my dressing room? Did he know my passcode? That was the only way anyone could have unlocked my phone without using my face to do so.

Fuck, fuck, fuck. Getting sent pictures and dead birds was one thing. But to know this person may have been close enough to touch my things—my phone that was my lifeline—was enough to make me feel light-headed.

Telling myself to calm down, I unblocked Jordan's number and was seriously glad I'd turned the phone to silent before entering the church earlier. Almost immediately, text alerts started blowing up my screen. By the time it was done, I had close to a thousand texts from Jordan.

My hurt and anger at him evaporated, and I looked up at him with regret. "I didn't block you," I whispered. "But..."

His brows shot toward the ceiling. "But what? If you didn't block me, who did?"

"I-I don't know." I was trembling so badly, my teeth began to chatter, and he started rubbing his hand up and down my arm in an effort to warm me. But that did nothing to help.

With a curse, he pulled off his suit jacket and wrapped it around my shoulders. "Baby—"

"I'll explain," I promised, keeping my voice low. "Just not right now. Th-this isn't the time or the place."

SEVEN

JORDAN

After I left Arella Christmas Eve, I went straight to my parents' house and told my dad I was done working in the Italy office. What I really meant when I said that was that I was done babysitting Letizia or anyone else. Aunt Gabs was right. I did need to make a choice, and I was tired of essentially being pimped out to stay in my father's good graces.

Jared Moreitti had been pissed at me when I bailed on college. I hadn't told him that I was bored to tears at school and that all I did was drink myself into a stupor just to get through the bullshit that was expected of me. The idiotic fraternity I'd had to join because it was my father's chapter. The classes that made my eyes glaze over because after spending most of my life shadowing my father in the business world, I already knew everything the professor was spouting on and on about.

My boredom had led me to drinking almost every day, and Mia had been scared I was developing a problem. It was because of her I'd realized just how unhappy I was with the way my life was going. Once that first semester was finished, I dropped out of college and told my father I was going to work my way up in one of his many companies.

I started out as an intern and quickly advanced to junior executive within a few years. If I'd stayed in Italy, I would have earned a VP position within the next six months. I worked my ass off to get to where I was, but fuck, it wasn't worth it if I was so unhappy there.

I hated having to go out to one club after another almost every night with people I disliked—or, in some cases, all-out hated. It disgusted me that I had to fight off Letizia and a few other clients' daughters because they thought I was going to fuck them, and then they got pissed when I wouldn't let them kiss me. The next morning, my face was usually all over the gossip pages and tabloids with those people. My entire personal life was front and center in that trash—or at least, what the world assumed my personal life was like.

But more than that, it killed me that I was so far away from Arella and that she probably thought the same as the rest of the world. That I was fucking all those girls I had to take out.

Christmas Eve, as I'd stood in my parents' living room, I told them everything. That I was quitting but would find a replacement and tie up any loose ends before I came back. My father had been pissed, saying I was flaking out on him yet again. First, with school. Now, with work.

But while he'd been raging on, my mother had just sat there and given me the brightest smile.

"Is this about Arella?" she finally murmured when Dad lost steam and eventually shut his mouth.

"I love her," I confessed. "And this distance thing is killing me."

"You have to be fucking kidding me." Dad had started

up again. "This is over some girl? You're going to give up everything you've worked for the past five years over some...some..."

Mom jumped to her feet, but without her cane, she stumbled, and Dad and I both moved to steady her. When Dad grasped her hips, she'd slapped his hands away angrily. "I want you to think about the mistakes you made in the past, Jared. I want you to remember how you broke me and went on about your life while I had to face one nightmare after another. Alone. And when you realize what a fucking asshole you are being to our son right now, I want you to apologize to him."

"*Dolcezza*," he whispered in a choked voice. "I..."

"Just don't," she'd told him quietly as she'd turned to face me. "Whatever you want to do, I'm behind you one hundred percent. I know Arella means a lot to you, and I realize that the things you've been..." She paused and gritted her teeth. "You've been asked to do things that have put you in a position that might make her think you don't care as much as you do. Do what makes *you* happy, Jordan. That is all I've ever wanted for you." As she'd picked up her cane and started out of the room, she called over her shoulder. "You can sleep in the guest room, Jared."

"Fuck," he'd muttered, scrubbing his hands over his face as he watched her walk away. When she was gone, he turned to face me. My father and I had never been close. He was a good dad but too much of a hard-ass at times for us to really connect. He'd never expected me to come along.

After Mom's accident, she was told she would never have children, so my birth had freaked them both out. I suspected my dad resented me a little because, for one, I had put my mom's life in danger during her pregnancy. For another, she always took my side.

"She's right," he'd said after standing there glaring at me for several long moments. "I made mistake after mistake with her. I don't want you to go through that, son. Any more than I want you to put this Arella girl through what I did your mom. If coming home is what will make you happy, I'll find you something in one of the companies here."

"No," I told him point-blank, and he'd blinked at me in confusion. "I mean, no, I don't want to work for you or one of the companies you own. I've got my own plans."

"But this is your legacy, Jordan. Everything will be yours one day."

That had been all he and my uncle Ricco had ever talked about. Ricco and his wife had never been able to have kids of their own. Eventually, they had adopted two little girls, but neither of them had wanted anything to do with the family business. I was expected to take over everything in time. A billion-dollar empire that the Giordano family had created. All of it was mine, and I didn't want any part of it.

"I'll take over when the time comes, but until then, I have projects of my own I want to work on."

For the past six weeks, I'd been working nonstop to finish any open projects and get everything ready to turn over to my replacement. The entire time, I'd tried tirelessly to reach Arella. When she wouldn't answer and I finally realized she'd blocked me, my first thought was to fly home and make her talk to me. Whatever made her pissed at me enough to block me, I would make it right.

But then a few projects I was wrapping up hit snags, and I had to make the choice to wait to talk to Arella about what was wrong, or put those projects on hold and delay my departure from the company that much longer.

Now, as I looked down at my girl and saw the haunted

look in her beautiful eyes, I realized I should have just said to hell with the projects. The way she was shaking so hard her teeth chattered told me something was wrong. I could see she'd needed me, and I wanted to kick my own ass for not having been there for her.

When the service ended and everyone filed out of the church to get into the line of limos to travel over to the graveside service, I held Arella back. My parents coming to this funeral should have been enough to show our respects to Remington Sawyer, but I had another reason for attending. His grandfather and my dad had done business plenty of times in the past, and I'd even worked with Remington on a couple projects over the last few years.

I'd known Arella would most likely show up since her cousin had been married to the man. She'd been late, something I'd expected because Arella had never been on time to anything a day in her life. I'd waited in the limo until I saw her enter the church then followed after her, knowing if she was still pissed at me, it was the only way I could get her to speak to me.

Having ridden with my parents, I guided Arella to her car that was waiting in the church parking lot instead of the line of limos. No one tried to stop us, but they probably figured I would just drive her over to the cemetery.

There was no way I was putting her through that, though. Not with the way she was still trembling against me.

I took her keys as I opened the passenger door and helped her sit. Leaning in, I fastened her seat belt and then pressed a kiss to her forehead before straightening. "I'll get you warm, baby," I promised.

"I'm not cold," she denied, but she pulled my jacket around herself a little tighter.

Her car was so tiny and I was a tall man, so I had to practically fold myself behind the wheel. It had been uncomfortable as hell sitting in it Christmas Eve, but I'd sat there anyway, desperate to see her.

The limo procession filed out onto the road, but when I went to follow, I turned left instead of right with the others. Arella sighed but didn't stop me. "I need to see Cathryn. Could you drive to her office?"

"Your agent?" She nodded, and my hands tightened around the steering wheel. "Baby, I need to talk to you. Can't this wait until tomorrow or later in the week?"

"Please, Jordan," she whispered. "It's important. And then I can explain what has been going on."

Releasing a heavy exhale, I gave in. "You're going to have to tell me where to go."

She sat quietly in the passenger seat, giving me directions every few minutes. Every time I glanced at her, I saw that she looked a little more fragile, and no matter how high I cranked the heat in the car, she still shivered like she had hypothermia. When I grasped her hand to entwine our fingers, she felt like a block of ice.

"Arella, tell me what's wrong," I commanded, lifting her hand to my lips.

"I didn't block your number."

"Yeah, I heard you before." My jaw hardened. If it were anyone else, I would have called them a liar and just made her tell me why she was playing games with me. But this was Arella. I knew she wouldn't do something like that. "If you didn't, though, who did?"

"I-I don't know," she muttered.

I stopped for a red light and glanced at her. She was looking down at her phone in her lap, her face pale, locks of her glossy dark hair falling forward. She appeared so fragile, as if the slightest wind would knock her over. In all the years I'd known and loved this girl, I'd never seen her like this. She was normally so strong, a fighter.

"Turn left up ahead," she instructed.

It wasn't long before I was pulling up in front of a tall building. After parking, I got out and walked around to open Arella's door. She was still shivering, and I tucked her close as we walked inside.

Cathryn Schneider's office was on the fifteenth floor. When we walked in, a receptionist lifted her eyes from a computer screen and smiled. But when she saw the look on Arella's face, she grabbed the receiver on her desk. "Arella Stevenson just walked in." After a moment, she hung up and gave us a tight smile. "Go straight back."

My girl led the way into her agent's office. Cathryn, an older woman with a short blond bob, stood as we entered and came around to embrace Arella. "Did something happen?" she questioned as soon as she stepped back.

Arella held out her phone. "Someone blocked Jordan's number in my phone, Cathryn. I...I think it was him."

The agent released a harsh sigh and took the phone from her. "Let me call Kirtner. Have a seat, doll." Her gaze lifted to me. "You too, cutie."

I guided Arella over to the leather couch against the wall and sat beside her. "Him who?" I asked her softly while Cathryn spoke to someone on her cell.

Arella sucked her bottom lip between her teeth for a moment before releasing the tortured flesh, causing it to plump. Unable to stop myself, I traced my thumb over it, making her mewl in pleasure.

"Him who, baby?" I repeated when she just sat there, staring up at me.

"My stalker," she breathed.

My blood turned to ice at those two words, and I pulled her onto my lap. "Tell me everything," I ordered.

EIGHT
ARELLA

I FELT LIKE I WAS HAVING AN OUT-OF-BODY EXPERIENCE as I sat on Jordan's lap and told him everything the creepy stalker had done to date. The boxes with the pictures, the lotion, the dead birds. Now, it seemed he'd gotten even closer than I'd imagined, and I was scared.

If he'd been in my dressing room while I was at work, that meant I might actually know this person. It could be someone I worked with, someone I saw regularly. Someone I spoke to, laughed with, perhaps even hugged.

That last thought caused me to shudder, and Jordan touched his lips to my temple. One of his large hands rubbed up and down my back, while the other kept hold of my thigh, locking me in place on his lap. Like this, I felt safe. Protected. Loved...

I shook my head at that ridiculousness, but I buried my face in his chest. I knew he didn't love me, but at least he cared enough to worry about me. Wanted to keep me safe from the man who was trying to freak me out. A man who might even want to hurt me.

Of all the people in my contact list, why had he blocked Jordan? Why not any number of other people? Hell, I had two ex-boyfriend's numbers in there, but when I'd peeked at them and a few other numbers on the drive to Cathryn's office, none of them had been blocked. Only Jordan.

It just didn't make sense to me.

"Detective Kirtner is on his way," Cathryn announced as she dropped her cell phone onto her desk. "He's going to take your phone and have his people look it over."

I could only nod as I sat there, my body slowly absorbing Jordan's heat. I'd never been so cold in my life, but I barely noticed. It was as if my entire body had gone numb. But as his heat began to invade me, I realized just how scared I really was.

There were people who thrived off feeling fear. They liked the adrenaline rush they got from watching horror movies or going to haunted houses. Mom and Aunt Harper loved that stuff, but I'd never enjoyed it. It made me mad when people tried to jump out and scare me. I'd almost ripped all of Nevaeh's hair out once when she'd hid in my closet and jumped out to surprise me one night when we were younger.

As the numbness dissipated, flashes of everything I'd been put through the past two months filtered through my mind, and my blood started to boil.

I couldn't remember ever being so pissed off in my life, and I jumped to my feet. Jordan tried to pull me back onto his lap, but I slapped his hands away and began to pace angrily. Maybe it was his nearness making me feel safe, but all the fear this motherfucking stalker had forced me to feel for weeks was gone. All that was left was the anger.

From the corner of my eye, I saw Cathryn lean back

against her desk and cross her arms over her chest, a smirk teasing at her lips.

"Shut up, C," I snapped at her, knowing exactly what she was thinking.

"I was beginning to wonder if this bastard had turned you into a scared little kitten. I mean, seriously. It was just a few little boxes with pictures of some guy spanking the monkey. Yeah, okay, so those little birds dying like that was sad. I may have shed a tear or three for them. But I didn't think it was enough to get too worked up over. Honestly, if you saw some of the fan mail my people have to go through for you on the regular, you would think this is all pretty tame." She tapped her manicured nails on her arm in time to some tune only she could hear. "Glad to see I was wrong and that fiery tigress I adore so fucking much was just beneath the surface. So, while I have you here, what did you think of that script I sent over?"

Jordan snarled—actually snarled—as he jumped up. "She obviously has reason to be scared. Some lunatic is stalking her. And now she discovers that he may have done shit to her phone? He was that fucking close to her." He stabbed his fingers through his hair, disheveling it in a way I'd always wanted to.

Watching him, I felt my fingers tingle to run through those dark strands, and I realized I was actually jealous of his own hands. Shaking off the feeling, I returned to pacing.

"He was that close..." he repeated. But there was something in his voice that had me turning to glance at him again, only to find his tormented eyes watching me intently. With a curse, he pulled his phone from his pants pocket. "I'm calling Mia. You're getting a full detail of security right now."

Of course, he would call Mia. Rolling my eyes, I

stomped over to him and snatched his phone out of his hands. The call hadn't gone through yet, and I quickly disconnected before she could answer. Two seconds later, a text came in.

Mia: ***You okay?***

I shot back a quick "Fine, talk later" reply and shoved the phone against his chest. "If I wanted an entourage of security, I would have told my sister, and Braxton would have taken care of it for me."

"Then why the fuck haven't you?" he demanded angrily.

"Because I don't want my parents to stress over this!" I exploded. "It's just some dumbass trying to freak me out. Which, I admit, I was. But now, I'm just pissed off."

His phone rang, but he tossed it onto the couch across the room and cupped my face in his hands. "Baby, you are getting security."

"No, I'm not." I pushed his hands away and focused on Cathryn, who was watching us like we were her new favorite soap opera. "When will Detective Kirtner get here?"

"He's on his way, doll. Shouldn't be too long." She got a text and picked up her phone to answer it.

"Arella, listen to me," Jordan caught my wrist in his hand and tugged me around to face him once again. His eyes looked wild, his chest heaving, and I hated how much it affected me. How much I wanted to press up against him and feel his hardness as I gave him another reason to look so exerted. "If this guy gets within a mile of you again, I'm going to kill him. You need security, if for no other reason than so I don't lose my fucking mind."

"I said no."

"Your parents don't have to know. I'll talk to Mia. We'll

do it all discreetly. No one but us, her, and Barrick have to know." When I just shook my head, he jerked me against him. My free hand pressed against his chest to steady myself, and I felt how hard his heart was pounding. "Please, baby. I'll take care of everything. Drake and Lana won't be aware of anything."

"No," I repeated. "And if you can't respect that, there's the door."

"You goddamn stubborn girl," he growled. Releasing me, he took two steps back before raking his fingers through his hair once again. He inhaled deeply and slowly released it, as if trying to calm himself down, but it didn't seem to work, so he did it again. "Fine. You don't want security, then be prepared to have me shadowing you day and night. Twenty-four seven."

I snorted out a laugh. "Yeah, okay."

His dark eyes narrowed. "Why the skepticism?"

"You'll be back in Italy no later than next week," I reminded him.

Jordan shook his head. "I'm home full time now."

"Really?" I felt my cheeks begin to warm at how happy his affirmative nod made me, and I quickly came up with another reason why the thought of this guy spouting nonsense about being my constant shadow was ridiculous. Really, there were hundreds, but as I stood there staring up at him, not a single one of them came to mind.

"So, you're going to stay at my apartment with me?" I threw at him instead. "I don't have a spare bedroom, and my couch is too hard to sleep on." He'd complained about how uncomfortable it was every time he'd come to my place. Which, admittedly, wasn't all that many times, but every single time, he'd had some wisecrack to make about my adorable—albeit more for decoration than comfort—couch.

He cocked his head to the side, gazing at me long and hard before grinning. The wicked hunger I saw deep in his eyes made me burn as his voice caressed my entire body. "Baby, if you think I'm not sleeping right beside you so I know you're safe, you're out of your mind."

NINE

JORDAN

My girl stared up at me with shock and need in her pretty blue-gray eyes for a long moment before smirking. "Sorry, I only sleep with guys who introduce me to their mothers."

Jealousy struck me in the gut, and I took a step closer to her. I bet she'd met fucking Lyle's mother. The thought pissed me off so much I wanted to punch something. "You've met my mom. She even went to your eighteenth birthday party."

Her smirk disappeared, and I saw something that looked like hurt flicker across her face before she quickly hid it. "Yes, but *you* have never introduced us. I don't share my bed with anyone who doesn't think I'm good enough to meet his mother."

"How many guys have shared your bed, Arella?" I gritted out. I needed to know how many, and their names, so I could fucking kill every last one of them. I would start with Lyle and work my way down the list.

Her eyes flashed fire at me. "How many girls have shared yours?" she countered.

Fuck, of course, she would turn it around on me. "Ever, or this year?"

"It's only February, but I'm sure the number is still a high one for the year alone," she sassed, but I saw the jealousy she wanted to hide before she lowered her lashes.

"Zero," I informed her, and her eyes narrowed on me. "My number for the year is zero." It was zero for the previous year as well, but she didn't look as if she believed me for the current year, so I didn't mention it.

"Huh," she muttered skeptically. "Well then, there you go. You have my tally for the current year as well."

"I want to know your total," I bit out. I *needed* to know how many motherfuckers had touched what was mine, but at the same time, I wasn't sure if I could handle knowing.

"You first," she countered, quirking a brow as if she were amused. She could read my jealousy because I sure as hell wasn't trying to hide it. "You tell me yours, and I'll tell you mine."

A throat clearing brought me back to the here and now, reminding me that we weren't alone. Cathryn's gaze was still on her phone, but she was obviously listening in. "Just an FYI. Kirtner texted me to say he's about five minutes away." She finally lifted her gaze from the screen. "I'm just going to step out and wait on him. Give you two a moment to sort out your...sleeping arrangements."

I waited until the door clicked closed behind her before speaking again. "When we're done here, we can stop by my place so I can grab some clothes."

She huffed in annoyance. "I told you I don't sleep with guys who haven't introduced me to their mother. It's my number one rule for sharing my bed with anyone."

"Then we'll stop by your place and grab you some things. We can sleep in *my* bed. Problem solved. No rules broken." Those pretty eyes narrowed on me yet again, but before she could blast me with her verbal abuse, I touched my thumb to her lips. They were so soft and full, and I couldn't help fantasizing about them wrapped around my cock. "Why is it so important that I introduce you to my mother when you have already met her? It makes no sense to me."

"You're right," she surprised me by saying, but just as I began to relax, she detonated her bomb. "It is a stupid rule to have. How dare I have standards and believe if I'm not important enough to a guy to be introduced to his mom, I shouldn't let him touch the sacred temple that is my body?"

When put in that perspective, I got exactly where she was coming from. But why the hell did she need me to introduce her to my mother when they already knew each other? Fuck, her parents and mine had been friends for years. Maybe they were not exactly the closest, not like her parents were with the Armstrongs, but my parents still respected Lana and Drake and always attended any gathering they were invited to by the Stevensons.

I'd never personally introduced a girl to either of my parents before. Not even Mia. Her mom and mine were good friends. Growing up, they would always make plans to have lunch or go shopping together, while leaving Mia and me home with one of our dads.

But then, I saw the hurt Arella couldn't completely hide, and I knew this was something important to her. Even though I didn't fully understand her need for me to introduce her to Mom, I wasn't going to fuck up with Arella any more than I already had.

"Steak or Italian?" I asked, pulling up my mother's contact information in my phone.

"What?" she muttered with a deep frown.

"Dinner tonight. Would you prefer steak or Italian?" I was already typing out a text, but Arella remained quiet. Lifting my head, I saw her standing there just watching me like she didn't understand the question I'd asked. "You want me to introduce you to my parents, so we'll all have dinner tonight."

"No, that's okay," she said quietly before turning to walk over to the wall of windows behind Cathryn's desk. "Maybe you should just head to Violet's. I'm sure your parents are still there, and I wouldn't want to keep you."

Biting back a curse, I sent the text and then pocketed my phone. I walked up behind her and wrapped my arms around her tiny waist, lowering my head to kiss her exposed neck. Feeling her shiver, I smiled against her flesh before nipping at it with my teeth.

"I told Mom to make reservations at her favorite restaurant here in LA," I murmured close to her ear. "As soon as we're done here, we'll stop and get you a new phone and then drop by your apartment to get your things." When she didn't respond, I sank my teeth into her neck, making her whimper and writhe against me. "Tell me you're going to come home with me," I commanded.

She remained tight-lipped, and I sucked on the sweetness of her skin, marking her. The way she responded only made me ache for her more. Her hips rolled back against me, rubbing over my hard cock, teasing me to the point of madness.

I lifted my head and shifted my hips, trying to readjust myself so I didn't cripple my dick. The action brought me back to our surroundings, and I pressed my forehead to the back of her head as I tried to get my body under control.

"Arella, we're staying at my place." The more I thought about it, I didn't want her to go back to her place alone. If this stalker knew where her parents lived, then he must have known her address as well. No fucking way was I going to let her stay there. "Stop being stubborn," I gritted out when she remained mute. "If you won't let me get you a bodyguard, then I will be your personal security."

Her continued quiet worried me, and I turned her. Grasping her chin between my thumb and forefinger, I tilted her head back until our gazes locked. "What's wrong?" I rasped out when I saw the glitter of tears in her eyes.

"Nothing," she lied and pulled away from me. As she walked away from me, the door opened and Cathryn returned, followed by a man in a suit who I assumed was the detective they had mentioned earlier.

Cathryn handed over Arella's phone, and the man messed with it for a moment before focusing on my girl. "Miss Stevenson, I would like a list of everyone you come into contact with at work. Even if you don't personally speak to them, I want their names."

Her brow wrinkling in concentration, she gave him a long list of everyone she saw on set for her drama. It took a while because there were a lot of people she came into contact with at the studio. The detective took notes on them all, including adding what each person's job title was. That Arella knew so many names of the people she worked with made me fight a smile. She was so kind that she made time to speak to everyone, no matter if they were a makeup artist, director, sound tech person, or even a cleaner.

It was refreshing, but also cause for concern. Any of those people she was so friendly with could be the creepy bastard stalking her.

Once the list was complete, Kirtner put the phone in an evidence bag and labeled it. "I'll have the tech guys do some tests, see if they can find any spyware apps or anything that might give us a lead as to who might be doing this. I suggest getting a new phone and a new number." He gave her a stern look. "But only give the number to people you absolutely trust. This guy hasn't tried to reach out to you with a phone call, but that doesn't necessarily mean he doesn't have your number."

"Yeah, okay. I understand." She wrapped her arms around herself. "Thanks for all your help, Detective."

He pulled a card from his jacket pocket. "I want you to have my contact information in case you need to get in touch. If you need anything, just give me a call. You said you think the blocking of Mr. Moreitti's number happened before Christmas, and you haven't had any new packages delivered since before you took your trip. I want to think that this guy got bored and gave up, but I'm also realistic. Stay vigilant."

Arella hesitated before taking the business card from him. "So, you don't think I need personal security?"

He lifted a shoulder in a half shrug. "For you, I would suggest an entire entourage of personal security. But that's because Cathryn has shown me some of your other fan mail, and I've seen how some of your followers have tried to ambush you at award shows." His keen eyes turned to me. "But that is your choice. I won't force the issue if it isn't something you're comfortable with. At least not at this time."

A phone going off had the detective pulling out his cell. Annoyance twisted his face. "Another case needs my attention," he announced but glanced at Arella again. "Remember, if you need anything, just give me a call."

She nodded. "Thanks again," she told him with a tight smile.

Ten minutes later, we were back in her car, and I was driving us to pick her up a new phone. She was still being too quiet, but I didn't want to argue with her, so I didn't force her to tell me what was going through her head.

Parking in front of my cell carrier, I turned off the car and got out. I walked around to the passenger door, opening it for her and offering her my hand.

"This isn't my carrier," she said as she glanced at the building.

"No, it's mine. I'm adding you to my plan." Taking her hand, I entwined our fingers and tugged her toward the front door.

"I don't need to be added to your plan," she complained. "I can pay for my own phone and anything else."

"I'm aware of that," I grumbled, opening the door. "But I want your phone connected to mine." Fuck, I wanted everything of hers connected to me.

She rolled her eyes. "Jordan, this is ridiculous."

"Do you want the same phone you had?" I asked as we waited for assistance. "It was the newest iPhone, right?"

She sighed heavily but nodded. "Yes, the one that was just released a few months ago."

"Okay, what color?" When a sales associate approached us, I told her what we wanted and that I wanted to add the line to my plan. It took barely fifteen minutes to get it all sorted, and while I paid for everything, Arella was already texting her new number to her parents.

I didn't imagine that just because she gave in so easily over the phone that she would do the same on everything else. It was a minor win, and I still had too many major battles to go.

Like getting her to move in with me. Permanently.

TEN

ARELLA

I DIDN'T ARGUE WITH JORDAN. NOT ABOUT THE PHONE. Or stopping by my place to get a few things. Or even about going to dinner that night.

Because I knew they were just words to him.

In a week, I would switch the phone over to my own carrier and keep the number and the new iPhone. He would get bored with me and I would be right back at my place, so I didn't bother to pack more than a few changes of clothes, toiletries, and my makeup bag.

As for dinner with his parents, I knew something would keep that from happening, so I didn't feel even a flicker of nervousness like I would have had I thought for even a second that would become a reality. Either Jordan would come up with some excuse that kept us from going, or his parents would. I was nothing more than one of their son's friends, not even important enough to be elevated to his best friend over the years. Really, I was no one to the Moreittis, so why would they want to take time out of their busy lives to have dinner with me?

That theory was proven correct when we walked into

Jordan's apartment and his phone alerted him to a text. As he tossed his keys into the beautiful decorative bowl that sat on his entrance hall table, he pulled his cell from his pocket and grunted as he read the message.

"My mom has a migraine," he said as he followed me into his living room, where I was already making myself at home. "Dad is taking her home so she can sleep it off. But they're going to let me know when a good day is to have our dinner."

The sudden lump filling my throat made me realize a small part of me had been holding out hope that I was wrong. Pushing back the sting of tears, I averted my face so he wouldn't see my weakness until I knew for sure I had myself under control.

"Okay. The rest of my week is pretty full, though." Not that I wouldn't have changed my plans if I thought Jordan's parents really did want to meet me. But they didn't.

I knew he didn't understand my need to have him introduce me to his mother. Honestly, I didn't fully understand it either. Maybe I wanted to know how he would introduce me. They knew who I was, so it wasn't like he even had to make an actual introduction. Yet, I yearned to know if he would tell them I was just his friend—or something more.

I rolled my eyes at that silly fantasy. Of course, Jordan and I were only friends. Maybe he wanted something a little more, like friends with benefits, but I would've had to be the most gullible person to walk the earth if I thought for even a minute that he would ever want anything more with me—or any other girl, for that matter.

"Since dinner with the parentals is postponed, what would you like to eat?" he asked as he sat down beside me on his couch.

Unlike mine, his couch was plush and so comfortable I

could have happily slept there for eternity. It was masculine, yet still decorative, and definitely something I would have picked out for him if I'd put the room together at his request. But his mom and Mia had helped him decorate his apartment when he'd moved in.

Not that he stayed there often. He spent so much time in Italy for work, the place was rarely lived in. But a cleaning service came in several days a week to make sure the place didn't get dusty, and the fridge was stocked in case he returned home on short notice.

When I didn't answer, he shifted, causing his thigh to brush against mine. I kicked off my heels and folded my legs beneath me so he wasn't touching me so casually. That small, innocent contact was distracting enough.

"Do you want to go out, or should I order in?"

"I don't feel like going out," I told him as I picked up the TV remote and started flipping through channels. "And I need to be at the studio at six in the morning, so I'm going to have an early night. I called in sick today so I could attend the funeral, so that will extend the filming of the finale."

He groaned like he was in pain. "That means we have to get up at four."

"No, it means *I* have to get up at four." I kept my gaze on the television as I channel-surfed, not really paying attention to what was on the screen, just needing something to look at other than him. "You don't have to do anything."

"I'm not leaving your side. You go to work, I'm going to be there." He snatched the remote from my hand and tossed it on the floor. Grasping my hips, he lifted me onto his lap and buried his face in my neck. "What scent is your shampoo?"

"Honeysuckle," I breathed, unable to keep from squirming as he pressed his nose into my hair and inhaled deeply. I could feel his hard-on pushing into my hip, and I swear, the thing was as thick as a tree trunk.

He thrust his hips up, making me want to turn and straddle him, take him deep and ride him all night long. I was about to give in, to hell with my rule, and pull him free from his pants. But before I could move, he lifted me and stood.

Breathing heavily, he turned me away from him. "Go shower. I'll order us some dinner."

Dazed, I picked up my overnight bag and walked toward his bedroom, weak-kneed. As I shut the door behind me, I realized he hadn't even kissed me, and yet my panties were drenched and my entire body ached as if he'd brought me to the edge of completion and left me hanging.

Shaking my head at how powerless I was where Jordan was concerned, I unpacked my pajamas and my toiletries. Taking both into the bathroom with me, I took a moment to look around the spacious master bath. The few times I'd been there, I'd never seen his personal bathroom.

The shower was huge, with clear glass, all-black tile on the walls, and a smoky white-and-gray tile on the floor. A rain shower fell from the ceiling, and it had a handheld shower head I could control the power of easily. The jets on the highest setting felt good on the knots of my neck and shoulders and made me cry out as I let it pulse against my clit.

But I didn't let it get me off. I wanted Jordan's touch, his tongue, his thick cock taking care of the ache he was responsible for. My meeting-the-parents rule be damned. It wasn't like that was going to happen anyway, and I needed to face reality and take him however I could get him for what little time we had together before he got bored and went back to Italy.

After I got out of the shower, I dried my hair and then walked out to the living room to find Jordan placing Chinese takeout boxes on the coffee table. He'd half unbuttoned his dress shirt, exposing his lightly hair-dusted chest and the tops of his abs. His sleeves were rolled up his forearms, something that had me gulping.

Some girls were into a guy's tight ass or even his calves. Oddly enough, it was a guy's forearms that made me lick my lips in appreciation. Although Jordan was the whole package with his well-defined ass, perfect calves, and basically leanly chiseled everywhere, he had forearms that made me want to trace my tongue over the veins that went up his arms.

And keep going over his entire body until I'd tasted every inch of him.

"I ordered extra egg rolls just for you," he commented as he started opening containers. "And yes, before you ask, I did get the honey chicken just so you could dip your egg rolls in the sauce."

"Dumplings?" I asked, and I bit my lip at how breathy my voice came out.

He lifted a container. "Dumplings with no dipping sauce because I know the smell upsets your stomach." He tapped a set of chopsticks still in their wrapper on the top of the soup. "Wonton soup as well."

That he remembered all my favorite Chinese foods caused butterflies to flutter in my stomach while I crossed to him and folded my legs under myself as I sat on the floor. He dropped down beside me, but instead of reaching for the food, he pressed his nose to the side of my head. "This is one of my favorite smells in the world," he muttered. "And it's going to be all over this place. I'm never going to want to leave this apartment now."

Needing to distract myself from his smooth lines, I reached for an egg roll and dipped it into the honey chicken. Taking a huge bite so I wouldn't be expected to talk, I licked the sauce off my bottom lip and chewed.

"Your phone was going off earlier," Jordan informed me as he picked up the container of noodles and thrust his chopsticks in to take a bite. "Who all did you give the new number to?"

I finished chewing before answering. "Just my parents, my sisters, and brother. Oh, and Palmer." Spotting the phone on the end table beside the couch, I grabbed it.

The text was from my mom. I'd told her I lost my phone, and since I'd been thinking about changing my number for a while because I'd been getting some annoying calls from the press, I'd gone ahead and taken care of it when I picked up a replacement phone. Having been at Violet's for the after-funeral gathering, she was just now getting back to me. Luckily, she was too distracted by what was going on with my cousin to really question me about my decision to switch numbers.

Mom: **Thanks for letting me know, sweetheart. Love you.**

I shot her a reply, telling her I loved her too, and dropped the phone on the floor beside me before grabbing a dumpling with my own chopsticks.

"You want wine?" Jordan asked as he picked up the bottle and poured himself a glass.

"No thanks." I didn't drink, not even wine. It wasn't because I wasn't old enough yet, but because my dad was a recovering alcoholic. It was mainly out of respect for him that I'd promised myself I would never touch a drop of alcohol, but also because, deep down, I was a little afraid I would use it as a crutch like he once had.

"Figured you would say that." He picked up the bottle of water and uncapped it before offering it to me. "Sorry, it's all I have besides the wine. I can order groceries if you need or want anything."

Wiping my mouth with a napkin, I took a small sip. "No, this is perfect. Thanks."

He picked up a dumpling and fed me half before stuffing the rest into his mouth. As he chewed, his eyes stayed glued to me.

"What?" I asked, wiping my mouth with the napkin again in case I had something on my face.

"Nothing," he murmured, leaning closer. "Just soaking in how beautiful you are." He brushed his lips over my cheek before skimming them down to my jaw. "And reminding myself I need to feed you before I drag you to bed and sink so deep into you that we can't tell where one of us ends and the other begins."

ELEVEN

JORDAN

Her soft hand touched my chest and pushed. I went willingly, grasping her hips as I fell onto my back and she straddled my waist. The food was forgotten as she leaned down and sealed her mouth to mine.

Our kiss Christmas Eve had haunted me, taunting me with her sweetness at all hours of the day and night. A reminder of why I was working so hard to get back to her. She was the sweetest thing I'd ever tasted, like sun-ripened raspberries. When I was a kid, raspberries were my favorite fruit, and all I wanted to do was gorge on Arella's mouth until I got my fill.

But I knew deep in my soul that I was never going to get my fill of this girl.

She scraped her nails down my chest as she rushed to get my shirt the rest of the way unbuttoned. When she reached the top of my pants, my belt buckle hindered her progress. With a frustrated little growl that was so fucking sexy my cock began to leak onto my thigh, she sat up so she could see what she was doing.

"Jordan," she whined so prettily. "Get your pants off. Now."

Letting her have complete control, I made quick work of my belt and then the button of my pants before kicking them off, leaving me in nothing but a shirt that was spread open and a pair of gray boxer briefs. When her gaze fell on the outline of my cock in my briefs, she sucked in a sharp gasp of appreciation.

She traced her fingers down my shaft over the cloth. Licking her lips, she looked up at me. "I've never been with anyone as big as you," she breathed.

Jealousy tried to rear its ugly head, but I forced it back. I didn't want to think about anyone but my girl tonight. No one was going to ruin this for us, especially not a ghost from her past trying to taunt me that I wasn't Arella's first.

After I pushed the material out of the way, my cock sprang free, the tip weeping for her attention. Taking her hand, I wrapped it around me, but her fingers couldn't completely connect as she fisted them. "Don't worry, baby. I'll fit in that sweet pussy."

A smirk teased at her lips. "I didn't think you wouldn't," she purred. "It's just going to be a tight squeeze." She tilted her head to the side, causing her glossy dark hair to fall over her shoulder. Her fist clenched as she pumped me. "Think you can handle that, big guy?"

In answer, a gush of jizz dripped from my tip and down over her small hand. "Only one way to find out."

Jumping to my feet, I lifted her into my arms and sprinted into the bedroom. The bathroom door was open, and I could smell her shampoo and body wash coming from there, causing my dick to twitch as the scents caressed me like a physical touch.

Placing her in the center of my bed, I grabbed her

pajama bottoms and tugged them and her panties off before reaching for her top. She wasn't wearing a bra, and her tits bounced as she braced herself on her elbows and looked up at me through her thick lashes.

I tossed my shirt across the room before stepping back and taking a moment just to appreciate the sight of her in my bed. Her skin had a slightly sun-kissed tone to it, making her blue-gray eyes stand out almost dramatically in her beautiful face. Every inch of her appeared to be silky soft, all the way down to her bare pussy that glistened with her need for me, making my mouth water to taste her nectar.

Catching hold of one of her ankles, I pulled her to the end of the bed and dropped to my knees. The scent of her arousal hit me, and I feasted my mouth on her drenched pussy lips.

Arella's fingers raked through my hair, tugging hard as she cried out my name. "Don't stop," she begged as I latched on to her clit. "Oh God, please don't stop."

I lifted my eyes to watch her face as I devoured her, wanting to imprint what she looked like when I made her come on my tongue. When it came to her pleasure, I'd give her whatever she wanted. All she had to do was ask, and I'd make it my life's mission to give it to her, no matter what it was.

This girl was mine to cherish and protect, to love until I took my last breath.

As I thrust two fingers into her quivering pussy, she came apart for me, and I nearly spilled onto the floor from the euphoria I saw shining out of her eyes. Giving her pleasure was addictive, and I licked and ate her through another before dragging her to the center of the bed and spreading her legs as wide as I could get them as I lined up my cock at her entrance.

She was still shaking from her last release, her pussy drenched. Her taste was still on my tongue, my face saturated with her juices, and I licked my lips, savoring her sweetness as I pushed into her.

"Jordan!" she screamed as I stretched her walls. She arched her back, opening herself up to me even more, and I sank even deeper into her wonderland.

"Fuck," I groaned as I bottomed out, my balls slapping against her luscious ass. My balls were already tightening up, telling me I was close, and I'd only been inside her for a matter of seconds. I couldn't ever remember blowing so fast, not even when I first became sexually active, but she felt so damn good, I was about to release deep into her.

She wrapped her legs around my waist tightly, holding me deep inside her as she adjusted to my invasion. Without my permission, my hips gave a shallow thrust, causing her to whimper.

"Baby, am I hurting you?" I gritted out, trying to hold back my release until I felt her milking it from me with her own orgasm.

"N-no," she said, shaking her head side to side as if she were in agony. "But it feels so good I think I might die."

Her walls clenched around my girth, making me see stars for a few seconds, and I couldn't help coming a little. "I need you to come," I groaned as I lowered my head and skimmed my lips over hers. "Because I'm about to embarrass myself if you don't."

"Yeah?" she breathed, clenching even harder this time, and I knew she was doing it on purpose. "So, you're a minute man?"

"Only with you," I said with a grunt, and she lowered her lashes, but not before I saw the pleasure my answer gave her. "You feel so fucking good, I can't seem to hold on to my restraint, baby."

To prove my point, I felt my cock release a little inside her. Not completely, just a micro-orgasm that had us both groaning.

"Jordan!" she cried out, her walls spasming around me and her nails slicing into my back as I spilled into her. "You're not wearing a condom!"

"Fuck, fuck, fuck," I chanted and pulled out of her. The action caused her to whimper and me to fight back an agonized growl. After being inside her, completely bare, all I wanted was to thrust back into her sweet heaven and never pull out again. Opening the top drawer of my bedside table, I reached in for a condom and made quick work of sheathing my cock. I was lucky there were even any in there. I hadn't bought any for at least two years, possibly longer, and those were for my place back in Italy.

Fuck, I couldn't remember when I'd last restocked my stash in this apartment.

As soon as it was in place, she pushed me onto my back and climbed on top of me. Straddling my hips, she grasped my cock in one hand and guided it into her. She felt so tight and wet, I fisted my hands in the covers beneath me to keep from pounding up into her. My cock stretched her all over again as she took me to the base, and we were both out of breath by the time she bent to kiss me.

"I've been tested. Everything was negative," she panted. "Just in case you were worried. I've never done this without protection."

"I wasn't worried," I assured her. "Fuck, babe, it was the last thing on my mind." I cupped the side of her face, tracing her bottom lip with my thumb. "I've never been so far gone that I forgot to put on a condom. This is a first for me too."

Her chin quivered. "I-I like that we get to share a first together," she whispered, and I felt a lump fill my throat.

"Me too, baby."

She started to ride me slowly, making us both forget about everything but how good it felt to be a part of each other. "I have a confession to make," she said in a breathy voice as she kissed down my chest. "I..."

"You?" I urged, my hands going to her hips to help her ride me.

"I've never actually come with a guy before." She lifted her head, and I noticed the pink that filled her cheeks. "Don't get me wrong. It felt good. But...I just couldn't get there."

Unintentionally, my fingers bit into her flesh, bruising her as my jealousy tried to ruin this moment yet again. "Doesn't seem like it's a problem now," I gritted out, trying to rein in my need to mark her entire body so the whole world would know she was mine.

"No," she moaned as her hips began to increase their pace. "Definitely not a problem now. I usually have to get myself off after, but I've already come twice and close to a third."

Cursing viciously, I flipped her onto her back and thrust into her so hard she screamed my name. "Arella, you are about to turn me into something I'm not if you don't shut the fuck up about sex with other guys."

Her nails stabbed into my hips, branding me. "And what is that?"

"A killer." Ducking my head, I caught her left nipple between my teeth and bit down. She rewarded me with her pussy clamping down on my cock so hard, I spilled a little.

Come filled the condom, but my cock was still rock hard deep inside her. "Because if you say one more word about the motherfuckers who touched you in the past, I will hunt each and every one of them down and put a bullet in their heads."

"Oh my God," she whined, her walls clamping and then spasming around me as she came. She dug her nails deeper, and I felt them pierce my skin, but it only revved me higher.

I lost control, pounding into her tight pussy so hard the bed frame slammed against the wall until I roared her name as I finally released. I felt something snap and knew it was the condom. With any other girl, I would have panicked. The risk of pregnancy, or that she might have lied and could pass something on to me, would have pissed me off, and I would've already been thinking of a way to get her out of my apartment.

Not so with Arella.

I knew she wouldn't lie to me about her health. But it was the thought of her belly swelling with our baby that had me falling on top of her and kissing her as my cock turned to steel all over again. Every time I'd thought about kids in the past, I'd literally broken out in a cold sweat. Now, I only wanted to see how much come I could pump into my girl to get her pregnant.

If she were carrying my baby, then everyone would know who she belonged to.

Did that make me a bastard? Probably.

Did I care? Not one damn bit.

"Jordan," she whimpered as I began thrusting my hips again. "You feel so good. I don't want it to end."

"Baby, you keep clenching that pussy like that, and I'll never be able to stop." I lifted just enough so I could pet her clit with my thumb.

"Shit!" she shouted. "I'm going... I'm... Jordan!"

The way she said my name when she was losing herself to the pleasure I was giving her sent me crashing into another release. It was so powerful, I felt like my spine was going to snap. Trying to catch my breath, I rolled onto my side, taking her with me and pulling her head to my chest.

"I-I think the condom broke," she panted. "I feel so sticky."

Struggling to breathe, I kissed the top of her head. "It did. I'd say I'm sorry, but I don't think I am."

"Me either," she mumbled sleepily. "Maybe I'll care tomorrow."

"I won't," I told her honestly, cuddling her closer as I gave in to sleep. Maybe I should have been a gentleman and gotten something to clean her up, but I liked the thought of her smelling like me all night too much to even move. "But if you are, then feel free to slap my face."

The last thing I heard as I drifted off was her pretty giggle.

TWELVE

ARELLA

"Time to get up, babe."

I groaned and turned away from the sound of Jordan's voice. "Five more minutes," I garbled sleepily.

"You're going to be late for your last day of filming," he reminded me.

"Five more minutes," I whined. "You didn't let me sleep at all last night."

I heard his deep laugh, and it brought a smile to my lips. Even half asleep, that sound could make me ridiculously happy.

But then he snatched the covers away and slapped his huge hand down on my bare ass. The loud clap of flesh on flesh was kind of sexy, and that slight sting had my pussy gushing. I pressed my thighs together and moaned as my inner walls complained.

He really hadn't let me get much sleep the night before. He woke me countless times, making love to me until I couldn't keep my eyes open and then letting me nap before starting all over again. I was exhausted, and from the way my lady parts were complaining at the moment, I was fairly sure I was going to be walking slowly all day.

"Get your beautiful ass in the shower before I really do make you late." I felt the bed shift and then his warm breath on my naked back. When his lips touched my skin, I whimpered as goose bumps popped up along my entire body. My nipples were already diamond hard, and his kisses along my spine were doing nothing for the issue between my thighs.

I rolled over, tempted to say fuck it. I was late for everything. The day I arrived on time—or God forbid, early—for something was the day everyone who knew me would be terrified the world was actually ending.

I looked up at him through my lashes and spread my legs invitingly. Only for the next sound out of my throat to be one of pain. It seriously felt as if my insides were shredded. Pressing my knees together, I rolled onto my side in agony and curled into a ball.

I had a high pain tolerance, but right then, I felt like if I had to move so much as a muscle, I would just give up. I'd had a good run, and if the way I left this world was because I'd had a night of the best sex of my fucking life, I was totally okay with that.

"Baby." Jordan's voice was soft and so damn soothing as he lifted me into his arms, carrying me into the bathroom. I felt his lips touch my brow, and I snuggled closer even though the lower half of my body was one huge, painful throb. "I'm sorry, Arella. I should have taken it easier on you last night. You were so tight. I should have given you time to recover, but I couldn't hold back after finally getting a taste of how good we are together."

I stroked my fingertips over his smooth jaw. Pouting, I let my head fall back so I could look up at his face. "I liked the scruff."

He kissed the tip of my nose. "I left friction burns on the insides of your thighs."

"So?"

"I don't like causing you pain." He set me on the sink then walked over to turn on the shower. With a frown, he glanced around the bathroom. "Maybe we should get another place. A house, perhaps? One with a huge bathtub for you to soak in."

My eyes had been half closed as sleep tempted me once again, but at his suggestion, they snapped open in surprise. "I'm sorry, I must have drifted off for a second there. What did you say?" No way he had just said he thought we should get a place...together? I mean, we'd only spent one night together. That didn't mean we should contemplate purchasing property.

He walked back toward me, and I found myself licking my lips as I appreciated the sight before me. Jordan in nothing but a pair of black slacks. His hair was already styled, so it was pushed back from his face. The scent of his cologne hit my nose, and my inner walls clenched involuntarily. There were scratches on his chest, along with teeth marks and love bites, and I couldn't help feeling a zing of possession that I'd marked him so thoroughly.

Too bad he would be wearing a shirt and no one would see how I'd branded him as mine. But I would remember every time I looked at him, and it drenched me.

"Where do you want to live? Closer to your parents, maybe? Or I think there were a few houses for sale in my parents' neighborhood. You would only be a few blocks from your aunt Layla and Emmie." He tenderly grasped my knees and carefully spread my legs as he stepped between them. "But I'm okay with wherever you want to live, babe."

"I, uh..." Shaking my head to clear it, I frowned up at him. "Is this because the condom broke last night?"

Something flashed in his eyes, and he moved one of his hands to touch my lower stomach. "Shh, don't talk about that, or I'll end up fucking your right here. And your sweet little pussy can't handle any more right now." Lowering his head, he brushed his lips over mine in a barely there kiss. "But to answer your question, this has nothing to do with the fact that I spent the entire night filling you with my come. I want to live with you. Wake up beside you every morning. Fall asleep with you in my arms every damn night. Hear your giggles in every room. Smell your scent on every surface. See your things touching mine in our closet."

The mental pictures he was painting in my mind had me melting. I liked this fantasy he was creating of us living together, but I wasn't sure if I could trust it. Maybe he wanted that now, but what about when he got bored?

The bathroom was filling with steam, and I gave him a tight smile as I pushed at his bare chest. "Let's revisit this conversation later," I suggested as I hopped down from the sink. My entire body protested the quick movement, but I bit back my groan of discomfort and kissed his chin. "My brain isn't completely awake, and I think I need to concentrate hard for a discussion this important."

He caught my hair in his hand and wrapped it around his wrist, tugging my head back so he could kiss me as deep and for as long as he wanted. Moaning, I melted against him, my nails biting into his chest and marking him yet again.

Lifting his head, he released my hair and swatted me on the ass. "Don't think you're getting out of this conversation that easily, baby. We *will* be talking about it again. Today, if I have my way."

Rolling my eyes, I walked into the shower to the sound of his deep laugh as he left the bathroom.

I got to the studio only slightly late, which, for me, was considerably early. When I walked into the makeup artist's room, her eyes grew round with surprise. "Are you that excited for the last day, dear?" the fifty-four-year-old woman who had been doing my hair and makeup for the past three years asked with a sad smile as I took my seat.

"Yes and no," I answered honestly. Sue had heard me bitch enough about my character to know I wasn't going to miss this show all that much once it was officially over. But she knew I would miss her and some of the other crew, although my fellow costars were definitely not on the list of people I wanted to hang out with in the future.

From the doorway, I heard a throat clearing, and I lifted my gaze to the mirror to find Jordan walking into the room. Sue turned, and I watched her eyes widen when she took in the sight of Jordan Moreitti.

"Sue, this is Jordan, my..." I bit my lip, unsure what exactly we were.

"Arella's boyfriend," he supplied, offering the woman his hand with that killer grin that never failed to make any member of the opposite sex weak in the knees. "Nice to meet you, Sue. Arella has told me so many good things about you over the years."

He was right about that, at least. I had praised my makeup artist from the first time I'd met her. Sue was the best. She could make the blond wig I had to wear look so natural, and my makeup always transformed me into someone I didn't even recognize. It was fascinating how a little makeup could make a person look so different when applied in certain ways. Sue had been working in the business since she was eighteen. She was so talented it was kind of scary the way she made me look so unlike my normal self.

Sue blushed, falling for Jordan effortlessly. It wasn't that I was jealous of Sue. With her gray-kissed blond hair and rounded curves, she was not only decades older than him, but very much not Jordan's type. Yet it irritated the hell out of me that he was turning on the charm and causing yet more of the female population to fall at his feet in worship. All while declaring himself my boyfriend.

Deciding to ignore him before I got pissed and started an argument with him, I pulled out my new phone and texted Palmer, asking her if she wanted to have lunch with me later.

Palmer: **Wish I could. My mother wants to have a meeting.**

I gritted my teeth, disliking Veronica Abbot even more. Usually when Palmer's mom said she wanted to have a meeting, what she meant was she wanted to set up her daughter with some random guy she hoped would cure Palmer of her homosexuality.

Me: **Call me later and tell me how that goes. Maybe we can get together this weekend.**

Palmer: **Defs, bestie. xo**

Sue finally stopped gushing over Jordan and came over to do my hair. I sat back, but my stomach started growling, and I wished I'd asked Jordan to stop at my favorite coffee shop on the way to the studio earlier. My stomach felt empty, and the single cup of coffee I'd had back at Jordan's apartment was not nearly enough to keep me functioning until lunchtime.

Jordan walked over to the makeup chair I was sitting in. Leaning back against the vanity where all Sue's brushes and makeup were spread out, he crossed his arms over his chest and gave me a long appraisal.

"What?" I asked when he just stood there, watching me.

Sighing heavily, he pulled his phone from his pants pocket and started typing. "Skinny vanilla latte and a vanilla bean scone?"

My stomach growled, making him smirk without lifting his gaze from his screen. "My assistant will be here momentarily with your breakfast. I apologize I didn't think to stop and feed you on the way."

"Adam?" The only assistant I knew he had was Adam, who worked with him in Italy. I'd never spoken to the guy personally, but I had heard him in the background a few times whenever Jordan called me from work in the past.

"No," Jordan told me as he pocketed his phone. "My replacement inherited Adam. I'm not happy that I have to get used to someone else, but so far, Taylor has kept my life pretty organized."

"Taylor," I repeated the name, trying to sit still so Sue could do her job without pulling me bald in the process, while also attempting to keep the sudden flare of jealousy out of my voice and off my face. That name was too unisex for me to know if it was a woman or a man. "You've been home like two minutes. When did you hire a new assistant?"

"I didn't. My mother did it for me." His phone buzzed with a new text, and he pulled it out. "I have a meeting in an hour or so for a potential project I want to work on, so she was on her way." He lifted his gaze from the screen. "They are out of vanilla bean scones. Blueberry muffin?"

"Just the coffee is fine." I turned my attention to my own phone in hopes of keeping my emotions out of my expression.

"You need to eat. Do you want a muffin or a breakfast sandwich?" When I kept my mouth closed, he growled something under his breath. "She'll get both. I don't want you to skip meals."

While he went back to texting Taylor, I rolled my eyes. Sue saw the action in the mirror and grinned. "A man who wants to feed you," she whispered and waggled her brows. "I would say that is a check on the pro list to keep him."

"Trust me, there are plenty of con checks already," I whispered back.

"What was that, babe?" Jordan asked, pocketing his phone once again.

"Nothing," I told him, lowering my gaze to my phone. "You said you have a meeting for a project?"

"Yes, I can't really talk about it just yet, but hopefully after today, I'll be able to make a decision." He snatched my phone from my hands. Sue was busy pinning my hair to my head so I couldn't move to grab it back as he stepped a few feet away. His eyes skimmed over what was on my social feed before placing my phone in his suit jacket pocket. "But once I do make a decision, I would like to run a proposition by you."

I lifted my brows curiously. "That depends. Are we talking a proposition that includes more evenings like last night, or me having to put on another stupid wig?"

His eyes darkened hungrily, but he quickly banked his need. "The former is a given. I don't think we need to negotiate the terms of that aspect of our relationship. Do you?" I grinned as he gave the wig Sue was about to place on my head a disgusted glare. "The latter...I would never ask you to wear a wig when I love all that glossy dark hair, baby."

"But it does involve a part in whatever project you're contemplating?" He shrugged. "Huh. Well, I'm willing to give it consideration. I haven't committed to a role in anything yet, but I have been offered several that require a decision in the next few weeks."

Sue secured the wig in place, and I instantly wanted to start scratching my head. Thank God this was the last time I would ever have to put the damn thing on.

"I think I can outdo any contract you've already been offered," he informed me with a wink.

"Oh, I'm sure you could," I purred. "Let's table this convo until you know more. Then we can discuss my demands, should I entertain your offer."

"Fuck," he groaned. "You just made the tediousness of contracts the sexiest thing ever. I'll hand over every penny in my bank account right now if you say yes."

A snort left me, causing Sue to laugh. "Why is that so funny?" the artist asked.

"He's a freaking billionaire," I informed her.

"Honey, if he's offering you that kind of cash in front of witnesses, you should sign on the dotted line now. No matter what the part is." Sue started brushing out the tangles in my hideous wig then stopped abruptly. "Except porn. Your parents would skin me alive if they knew I allowed you to agree to porn while I was in the same room."

"It's not porn," Jordan growled. "And I would kill anyone who even suggested she do that shit."

I tilted my head back, fighting a happy grin at the sight of the possessiveness in his dark eyes. "You've been awfully vocal about murdering people in the last twenty-four hours, Moreitti."

He placed his hands on the armrests of my chair and bent down until his lips were almost touching mine. "Shall we revisit the hit list I'm still tempted to start, beautiful?"

I kissed him quickly before putting my hand over his

heart. Feeling how hard it was beating against his ribs melted me. I loved that, with an innocent kiss, I could affect him so powerfully. "No one who you think should be on that list matters to me, so you should stop considering a life of crime and just kiss me. Because I don't want to think about my life with you behind bars."

"I'm going to assume I'm in the right place since you are here, Mr. Moreitti. Considering you didn't give me very detailed directions on where you would be in this maze," a husky female voice muttered before Jordan could kiss me.

He straightened, and the look of annoyance on his face made my disappointment that he didn't kiss me ease. "Her drink better be made correctly, or you'll be going back," he said coolly as he crossed to the door and took the drink carrier from her. Pulling a venti cup free, he offered it to me.

I glanced at the order sticker on the side of the cup, saw that it had been ordered exactly the way I liked, and took a sip. With Jordan no longer blocking my view of his new assistant, I gave her a quick once-over.

Dressed in a chic pantsuit that was molded to her curvy ass, with her short hair styled on the top and shaved on the sides, she was hot as hell.

Jealousy growing by the second, I took another drink of my coffee and discreetly watched Taylor. I noted that the way she looked at Jordan was with anything but interest. Considering the flippant way she'd greeted him, I was almost convinced she didn't even like him all that much. But when her light-brown gaze landed on me, interest flared. That had me openly appraising her.

She pushed the sleeves of her blazer up to her elbows, and I took in the tattoo along her forearm, causing my heart to lift with excitement.

The colorful heart within a heart, along with the heartbeat and the script "two hearts beating as one," was something I'd seen before. I'd gone with Palmer when she'd gotten almost that exact same tattoo.

My jealousy over Jordan having a hot female assistant evaporated, and I gave her a warm smile. "Thank you, Taylor. This is perfect."

"Of course, Miss Stevenson. Is there anything else I can do for you?"

"Actually..." I grabbed Jordan's jacket and tugged him closer so I could take my phone back. "Are you single?" I asked casually as I brought up Palmer's contact information.

"The fuck does that matter?" Jordan snarled, crushing the paper bag Taylor had just handed over. "You're not single, so her being single isn't an issue."

I bit my lip to keep the grin off my face. Maybe I shouldn't have been so ecstatically happy that he was showing signs of being just as jealous as I was, but I loved it.

"I'm single," Taylor informed me with a ghost of a smirk teasing her lips.

"Perfect." I hit connect and lifted the phone to my ear, waiting for my best friend to pick up.

"I told you I have a meeting with my mother," Palmer bitched. I knew just from that sentence alone that her mom had already said something to hurt her feelings. "I'll call you back."

"I'm looking at your soul mate right this second," I told her, and as expected, she shut up. "She has the same tattoo on her wrist that is on your hip."

"She does?" Taylor was beside me in the next instant, causing Jordan to snap at her. But when I shot him a glare, he closed his mouth and pulled my food from the bag he'd crushed. The muffin was a sad pile of crumbs, but the breakfast sandwich was thankfully intact.

"You have my attention," Palmer said after a brief pause.

"She's hot as fuck, Palms. I mean, damn." Taylor beamed at me while Jordan growled something about finding a new assistant ASAP. "That's okay, babe," I told him with a mock glare. "You fire her, and I'll hire her as my own."

His jaw turned to granite. "I take it back. She's the perfect assistant for me."

"No, no. I think she would fit me perfectly," I argued. "She's easy on the eyes and orders the best coffee. I've been meaning to get an assistant. Perhaps then I'll have more time for personal things. Like having a boyfriend."

"Are you actually playing tug-of-war over me right now?" Taylor asked with amusement thick in her voice.

I laughed. "Maybe. So, how about it? Want to work for the crazy actress? I come with a sexy BFF."

Jordan growled menacingly and stepped in front of me, blocking my view of Taylor. "I'll double your salary."

"Done," she accepted without hesitation. "Sorry, Miss Stevenson."

"It's fine. At least I got you a raise." Palmer made an annoyed sound in my ear, reminding me that she was still waiting. "So, lunch?"

THIRTEEN
JORDAN

Watching Arella work was one of my favorite things. I'd done it before in the past. Right after she started on this drama, I would stop by the studio to take her to dinner. I always came a little early so I could watch her filming a scene or two. The way she brought her character alive always gave me goose bumps.

The director knew my father, so he didn't give me any issues when Taylor and I stood off to the side watching. But when I spotted the man walking in, I realized time had gotten away from me. I was supposed to meet Garon across the lot in the executive offices over an hour ago, but watching my girl had made everything else escape my mind.

Garon Steel was one of several executives that owned Strive Studios. They were the third-largest production company in the business, and they mostly did television shows. But for almost a year now, Garon had been approaching me with an offer to come on board and for the two of us to take Strive in a new direction. He wanted to do a series of female villain action movies.

The idea had grown on me, and when he'd sent me a

rough draft of the script for the first movie, I'd finally decided to take a meeting with him. If I did, however, I knew exactly who should play the sexy little villainess. No one could pull off that feisty, sassy-mouthed vixen better than Arella.

The only issue was, she would be working with Garon.

Although he was her uncle, there had been no connection between her family and the man for her entire life, from what I understood. Cole Steel had turned his back on his son and ex-wife for whatever reason, and when he'd passed, he'd left everything to Lana and her children. I hadn't even seen Garon or his mother at Cole's funeral.

Arella worked for Strive with this drama, but she'd never had any dealings with her estranged uncle. Would she agree to take the role I knew would be perfect for her if it meant having to be around the man her family seemed to detest?

If she didn't, I would turn his offer down flat. But if she did agree, then I would put all the money the project needed into it.

Garon strutted toward me, and I was reminded of what a cocky bastard he could be. He had the same honey-brown eyes as his father and half-sister. The suit he wore was tailored to his lean frame. His hair was on the shaggy side, but stylish. I figured he dyed it, because he was at least five years older than Lana, and there wasn't a single gray hair on his head. I was several inches taller than the man, but he walked like the world had to look up to him.

As he neared, he stuck out his hand, and I shook it. Other than that greeting, we remained quiet as we turned our focus to the scene currently being filmed a few yards away.

When the director finally called "Cut," Garon cleared his throat.

"She's incredible, I'll give her that," he praised, then lifted his arm toward the door. "Shall we?"

I glanced over at Arella, who was busy speaking to the director. The man was listening intently to whatever she was suggesting and nodding along with his assistant. Taylor was nearby, watching in fascination and more than a little awestruck by what she was getting to see firsthand.

"Taylor," I called to her. She snapped to attention and rushed over to me.

"Sir?"

I nodded toward Arella. "Whatever she needs, make sure she gets it. I'm going to take this meeting alone."

"Yes, sir."

"I mean it. Whatever she needs." She promised she would stay close, and I followed Garon out the exit.

"How did you like the script I sent you?" the older man asked as we made the walk across the lot toward the executive offices.

"It has room for improvement, but for the most part, it kept my attention." We passed a few security guards in golf carts and several people with headsets attached to their ears. The place was bustling. Arella's show might have been ending, but there were many other projects the production company was filming.

"I've been talking to Montez about directing," he tossed out casually as he opened the door to the building.

My eyes widened. Scott Montez was an Oscar-winning director, and he had a knack for action films. Every production company in the business wanted him to direct their movies. Getting him wouldn't come cheap, but for this project, it would be worth it.

"He said he would think about it." Garon pressed his lips into a hard line. "If we happen to have a part for his wife."

I shrugged. "Shannon Stewart is a huge name."

"He also stipulated he wanted his daughter to write at least one song on the soundtrack and for his son-in-law's band to sing it." Garon rolled his eyes, and the action reminded of Arella's mom.

I shrugged again. "Kin St. Charles has some sick skills. Getting her name on any song is like an instant spot on the top ten charts. And Tainted Knights is probably the most popular rock band in the world. They sell out every concert eighteen months in advance. I don't really see what the problem is with any of those stipulations. If anything, they would only make the project better in every way."

We passed Garon's assistant and walked into his office. He shut the door behind us then motioned to one of the chairs in front of his desk. "Are you thirsty? I can have my assistant make us some coffee."

"I'm good," I told him as I sat down. I waited until he was seated before speaking again. "You seem irritated that Montez wants to include members of his family. Did you have other people in mind for the soundtrack and whatever role Stewart would play?"

"No. I just know that nepotism invites chaos and drama." He leaned back in his chair. "But I will admit that having all those names linked to this movie series will be cheap advertising. All we would have to do is drop their names into a few conversations."

"Exactly," I agreed. "Now, let's talk numbers."

He already knew I was only on board if Arella took the leading role. I was surprised he hadn't argued with me on that since there was so much animosity between him and his sister. If anything, he'd practically jumped at the suggestion of his niece playing such a major role in his movie.

By the time we concluded the meeting, it was lunchtime. Leaving him in his office, I walked back to Arella's studio. As I entered the building, it was to hear Arella speaking loudly.

"I just wanted to show everyone my appreciation for all your hard work over the past three years. Through everything, each and every one of you have been the real MVPs. My behind-the-scenes heroes," she told the group in front of her. Sound crew, cameramen, makeup artists, stylists, and other production staff were gathered around as they all looked at my girl adoringly. "I sincerely hope we can work together in the future. Now, please enjoy this farewell lunch Taylor was so sweet to set up for me at the last minute."

After everyone thanked her and gave her hugs, they got in line for a huge buffet set on tables along one wall.

While I watched and waited, Taylor came over to me. "Did you need something, Mr. Moreitti?"

"You did all this while I was gone?" I'd only been gone two hours, so I was impressed with how she'd pulled everything together so quickly.

"Miss Stevenson said she wanted to do something for the crew since no one else was showing their appreciation."

"Good work," I told her. "Keep this up, and I might triple your salary."

"Will my duties include helping Miss Stevenson as well?" she asked, sounding hopeful.

I turned a glare on her. "No, but it will include you finding her an assistant of her own. I want someone for her who is just as efficient as you are. But one who won't flirt with or eye-fuck her every chance they get."

Her lips twitched with amusement. "So, a gay guy?"

"I don't think I can legally stipulate that, but yes." My phone alerted me to a text message. Pulling it from my pants pocket, I saw it was my mother. "Get on that, Taylor."

"Yes, sir. Right away," she said with a light laugh.

As I sent a reply, I walked over to where Arella was speaking to a small group.

"Babe, we were supposed to meet Palmer ten minutes ago," I reminded her.

She quickly said goodbye to the others. As she turned around, I caught her around the waist and kissed her. With a happy sigh, she melted against me. "I take it your meeting went well?" she asked as we walked toward her dressing room.

"That depends on our conversation later tonight," I told her, letting my hand slip to her ass and rubbing my fingers over the fleshy globe. My cock hardened, pressing painfully against the zipper of my slacks. That effortlessly, she made my body respond. I stayed hard for her.

As soon as we were in her dressing room, I kicked the door shut. She glanced at me over her shoulder at the sound of the lock being flipped into place. "Take that damn wig off," I commanded, already undoing my belt.

She pulled it off then reached under her dress and pulled off her panties. I grabbed them and stuffed them in my jacket pocket. Wrapping my fingers around her wrist, I pulled her over to the couch and sat. One-handed, I undid my slacks and reached in to free my throbbing cock.

"I'll be easy," I promised as I took hold of her hips and lifted her until she was straddling me. I felt her pussy drip onto the head of my cock and groaned through my teeth to muffle the sound.

Slowly, she sank down on my shaft. "Is it wrong that the

pain makes the pleasure that much more intense?" she breathed at my ear.

My cock flexed inside her, causing her to whimper. "Nothing that makes you feel good could be wrong, baby."

As she moved her hips, riding me so well I saw stars, I strummed her clit. I wanted to linger, savor every second of her like this, but we were already late for lunch with her friend. When her breathing changed, I knew she was close. Two more pumps into her sweet pussy and she came apart for me.

"Jordan," she cried, her eyes wild as she jumped to her feet.

I growled at the loss of her and grabbed for her, but she only glared at me as she dropped to her knees between my legs. "You forgot the condom again," she scolded. "We need to be more careful."

"Babe—" But whatever I was going to say escaped my mind as she fisted the base of my cock and wrapped her lips around my tip. "Ah, fuck, baby."

Her hair was still pinned in place so the wig would sit seamlessly on her head. Cupping the back of her head, I urged her to take more of my length. Seeing the way her lips were stretched around my shaft, watching her cheeks hollow as she sucked me off, was enough to make my balls tighten. When the tip hit the back of her throat and I felt her swallow without pausing for breath, I exploded.

Her soft hand stroked me through the release, milking every drop of come from my cock. Pulling back, she licked her lips, making me want to bend her over and fuck her all over again.

Grinning wickedly up at me, she leaned forward and pulled her panties from my pocket. "To be continued," she murmured in a voice so sultry, my cock turned to stone.

Seeing my reaction to her, she giggled and kissed the tip before hopping to her feet. Stepping back into her panties, she fixed her dress and started pulling the pins from her hair. "Give me five minutes to make myself presentable, and then we can go."

I sat there watching her brush out her hair, and I half-heartedly stuffed my dick back into my pants. I could smell Arella on my clothes, and that made me smug as hell.

"We could skip lunch with Palmer and go home for an hour or two," I suggested. "Just send Taylor over to meet her alone. They won't want us around anyway."

She *tsked* me as she pulled her long dark hair up into a ponytail. Picking up her purse and phone, she crossed to the door. "Are you coming? Because I have no problem going without you."

Sighing heavily, I got to my feet. Her blue-gray gaze skimmed over me with banked hunger, and I growled at her in response. With a giggle, she took off running. Grinning to myself, I gave chase.

Fuck, but she made me happier than I could ever remember being in my entire life.

FOURTEEN
ARELLA

Palmer knew me so well that she already had drinks ordered and salads waiting on the table when we finally got to the restaurant. My tardiness was just something those who loved me accepted without complaint. I tried to be on time; honestly, I did. But things always just came up—or distracted me.

Luckily for me, I had understanding people who overlooked my shortcomings.

As we walked toward the table where Palmer was waiting for us, I could practically feel Taylor's nervousness. She'd asked me all kinds of questions about my bestie that morning and on the drive over. I'd shown her pictures of Palmer earlier and seen the interest in the other girl's eyes. Palmer was beautiful, with her rich, chestnut hair, chocolate-brown eyes, and killer curves. There was a small brown birthmark on her left cheek and a light smattering of freckles across her nose that only added to her beauty.

"Relax," I murmured so only Taylor could hear me. "Palmer is the sweetest, unless you piss her off." I paused and turned to face her. "Um, I really hope you don't have to see her pissed off before you two decide you love each other or not."

Taylor laughed. "I hope she doesn't have to see me pissed off before she can decide the same."

That made me giggle, causing Jordan to shift Taylor aside so he could put his hand at the small of my back. "Ladies, I'm starving. Shall we?"

I rolled my eyes over my shoulder at Taylor, who had to cough to hide her laughter. But his continued possessiveness was so damn sexy and adorable, I couldn't help pressing a little closer into his side as we walked. Our quickie back in my dressing room had been the most perfect last day of filming celebration I could have possibly had. Just remembering how hot he'd been for me, and how quickly he'd gotten me off, made my inner muscles pulse.

I'd been all too tempted to take him up on his suggestion to go back to his place for a few hours earlier. But I knew my best friend needed me, and that was the only reason I'd turned him down.

Palmer stood as we neared, and I could tell she was just as nervous as Taylor. I shot her a reassuring smile, knowing that she and Taylor were going to be perfect together. The more time I'd spent with Jordan's personal assistant that morning, that had become even more apparent to me.

Reaching Palmer, I pulled away from Jordan to hug my bestie. She kissed my cheek. "She's hot," she whispered before pulling away, making me wink at her in agreement.

"Palms, this is Taylor Holt," I introduced. "Taylor, Palmer Abbot."

Taylor offered her hand, which Palmer eagerly accepted. But after shaking, the two stood there holding hands, seemingly speechless. They had only spent a few seconds together, but I could already see the sparks flying between them, just as I'd known they would.

Pleased with myself, I took a seat at the table, and Jordan joined me. After another few moments, Taylor pulled out a chair for Palmer. "Thank you for ordering starters," Taylor told her as she took the seat beside her, putting herself right in front of me. "I'm so hungry."

"I would have ordered entrees too, but I didn't know what you like," Palmer said apologetically. "And knowing Moreitti, he would have just bitched at whatever I ordered for him."

I bit the inside of my cheek to keep from laughing when Jordan grumbled something under his breath. I didn't know why he'd always been so grumpy around Palmer. Secretly, I'd hoped it was because he was jealous of her. Whether it was because she was my best friend, or because she'd once had a thing for me, but still jealous. Although that was ridiculous, I'd still hoped.

Picking up the menu lying beside my salad plate, I opened it to skim through the entree selections. As I did, I stabbed a fork into a cherry tomato and ate it while letting the other two girls chat.

Jordan scooted his chair closer to mine and leaned over to examine my menu. "How about the salmon, baby?"

My stomach growled in approval. "That sounds yummy."

His nose nuzzled my neck. "Want to know what else sounds yummy?" He touched my leg, stroking his fingers up the inside of my thigh. "Taking you home and eating this pussy for dessert."

There was no way he could miss how his words made me quake. I still had to go back to the studio to clear out my dressing room, but other than that, I had nothing left to do there. Maybe I could have Taylor clear it out for me and go home with Jordan...

As that thought entered my head, our waiter appeared beside me. "Are we ready to order entrees?" he asked in a cheerful voice.

Jordan ordered for the two of us after Taylor and Palmer each gave theirs. The entire time, Jordan still has his hand on my leg, his sensual fingers teasing me as they skimmed up and down my inner thigh, coming closer and closer to my still-drenched panties.

After the waiter walked away, Jordan leaned in to whisper in my ear. "I can smell you on my slacks, baby. When you came earlier, you soaked me. I want to make you gush like that again. I want that scent everywhere. Want that sweet juice flowing down my throat as I eat you out."

Glancing at the other two out of the corner of my eye, I was thankful they were deep in their own conversation, their heads close together as they spoke to each other. Their smiles were shy but flirty, and I heard Palmer's giggle and knew she was besotted. Meanwhile, they were clueless that I was about to come just from Jordan's idle caresses and dirty words.

My legs began to shake, and I knew if he so much as flicked his finger over my panties, I was going to burst apart. Trying to control my breathing, I picked up my water glass in hopes of cooling myself down.

My phone ringing had me jerking. Jordan's eyes were full of heat as I reached for my cell. Seeing it was Sue, I answered. "Hey, Sue. I—"

"Someone destroyed your dressing room!" she yelled. "I was walking back from lunch and passed it. Girl, the place is a wreck. Thank God you weren't here, because whoever did that kind of damage probably would have hurt you if you had been."

Suddenly, I was trembling for an entirely different reason. "I'll be right there," I told her as I got to my feet.

"Okay, girl. Just hurry. I wasn't the only one who saw the mess. The director's assistant called security, and now the rent-a-cops and some of the execs are on their way."

Groaning, I ended the call and grabbed my purse. Palmer and Taylor looked up at me in concern. "What's wrong?" my best friend asked.

"Just an issue at the studio." I glanced at Jordan, who was already on his feet. He pulled out his wallet and tossed down several large bills. "Enjoy the rest of the meal. I'll call you later," I promised Palmer as he grasped my elbow, telling Taylor he would be in touch later.

He didn't speak again until we were in his car on the way back to the studio. "What happened?"

I grimaced. "I don't know for sure. Sue told me someone destroyed my dressing room and that security and the execs were on their way over to check it out." Heart racing, I glanced over at him. "Do you think this could have been...him?"

"I don't know, baby. Call that Kirtner guy and have him meet us over there," he instructed. Once he was on the road and I had my phone to my ear, he grasped my free hand. The way he gave it a reassuring squeeze kept me calm while I explained what was going on to the detective.

"You said it's your last day of filming?" Kirtner asked after I told him everything I knew.

"Yes."

"Maybe this guy is spiraling if he won't have such easy access to you every day," he mused. "It could make him more dangerous, Miss Stevenson. I'm only a few miles from the studio. I'll see you there."

Spiraling? What the fuck did that mean?

Shivering, I clutched at Jordan's hand as he changed lanes. Before long, he was pulling into my usual spot at the studio after being waved in past security. With his hand on my hip, we entered the building, and immediately, I saw that the place was in complete chaos.

Several people tried to stop me along the way, but I ignored them as we headed straight for my dressing room. A group of people was milling outside the room, with a member of security standing guard to keep them back. I heard loud, muffled voices coming from inside and pushed through the crowd to see what was going on.

Detective Kirtner was already there, standing in the middle of a group of executives in their expensive suits. My gaze skimmed over them, my jaw clenching when I spotted one particular man, but I pushed down my annoyance. Just because *he* was there didn't mean I had to speak to him.

The security guard tried to stop me when I would have entered the room. "No one is allowed inside," he informed me and started to put his hand on my arm.

"Back the fuck off. Touch her, and the last thing you ever see will be my fist in your face," Jordan snarled at him, causing the man to flinch before he stepped out of the way.

Jordan's loud voice had the group inside my dressing room turning to watch us. I walked in, my gaze traveling around the space. Everything was turned upside down. My mirror was shattered, the little vanity under it broken down the middle. The small chair that once sat in front of it was across the room, sticking out of the window. My couch was turned over, with the cushions spread around the room. The few personal items I'd kept there had been destroyed and scattered on the floor.

As I walked, my heels crunched on the broken glass of what used to be a bottle of my favorite perfume. The light floral scent filled the air overpoweringly, giving me a headache. Or maybe that was because my pulse was suddenly throbbing in my temples as my fear escalated.

"Is there something you want to tell us, Arella?"

My head snapped around at the almost accusatory tone in Winston Cline's voice. Winston had overseen my drama, so I'd worked with him more than the other executives. He was a man in his late fifties with a slightly pudgy middle and a comb-over that didn't fool anyone. Not even his five-thousand-dollar suit could distract from the fact that he looked beyond ridiculous with the way he styled his hair.

Squaring my shoulders, I lifted my chin and glared at the man down my nose. "It would seem I have a stalker. Big whoop. Everyone gets them."

"Yes, but you should have informed us so we could have boosted security and kept them alert. Not only was your safety in peril but that of everyone else on the property."

Remorse filled me, and my shoulders drooped. "You're right. I apologize. It was selfish of me not to consider the safety of the others."

"Relax, Winston, you fucking bag of hot air." I stiffened at the sound of *his* voice, my hands balling into fists at my sides.

I hate him. I hate him. I hate him.

"If she didn't think it was something to worry about, then she didn't do anything wrong," he continued. "No one was harmed, so relax and leave the girl alone."

That Garon Steel was defending me blew my mind, but it didn't soften me in the least toward the man who was my uncle in name only. He wasn't like Uncle Shane or Uncle Jesse. Not even like my honorary uncles, whom I adored. I despised Garon more than any other human being in the world. It was already making my skin crawl that I was in the same room with him, breathing the same air. But his voice was so similar to Pop-Pop's that it made my heart ache.

As if sensing my distress, Jordan touched my back. Just the feel of him, knowing he was so close and that I didn't have anything to fear as long as he was with me, helped me relax, and I finally looked at Garon. His brown eyes, so much like my mom's, were guarded as he met my gaze. But for a moment, he seemed to take in how close Jordan was to me, and I saw a flash of anger cross his face.

It was there one moment and gone the next, making me think I'd imagined the whole thing, but it still left me uneasy, and I stepped closer to Jordan.

"Detective Kirtner, did you find anything?" Jordan asked.

"Unfortunately, no," the man said, his eyes traveling dispassionately over the executives. "By the time I arrived, there were too many people in the room and the crime scene was completely contaminated. However, based on how destroyed this place is, I would say the stalker is escalating." He shifted his gaze to me, and I softened. "Miss Stevenson—"

"Call me Arella," I interrupted. "Please."

He gave me a grim smile. "Arella, then. At this point, I think it is better to err on the side of caution and employ personal security."

"I'll think about it," I lied. There was no way I was going to tell my sister about any of this. Nevaeh would freak out and blab to our parents, causing them to freak out in turn. And there was no way I could go to Barrick and

Braxton and expect Brax not to tell my sister about this. He would never keep something like this from her, and I wouldn't expect him to.

But I refused to be the cause of stress for either my mom or my dad.

FIFTEEN
JORDAN

From the moment we walked into Arella's dressing room, I'd been shaking. The place was destroyed. Not a single object was left intact, and I knew in my gut that if my girl had been there when the motherfucker had done this, she would have been a casualty as well.

Imagining Arella broken like the perfume bottle under my feet was a disturbing picture I couldn't erase from my mind.

I'd been concerned for her safety after she'd told me about the packages and then that she thought the stalker had messed with her phone. But this just shoved it in my face how dangerous the person who was obsessed with her seemed to be.

After nearly an hour of answering questions for both Detective Kirtner and the executive dickwads, I decided enough was enough. "I'm taking her home," I told Garon. We shared a look, his expression like stone, before he finally gave a firm nod.

Not that it would have mattered. I didn't need his approval to take my girlfriend anywhere. As we walked back to my vehicle, I shot a text to Mia. After seeing the way Arella shut down at the mention of personal security earlier, I knew it was going to be hard to get her to agree to it. She'd told Kirtner she would think about it, but I knew her too well not to be able to read that she was going to be stubborn about the issue.

Maybe if I could convince her Drake and Lana wouldn't find out, she would be more agreeable. But to do that, I needed Mia and her husband on board with a promise they wouldn't let the Stevensons know what was going on with their daughter.

Opening the passenger side door for her, I stopped her before she could slide into the seat. When she looked up at me inquiringly, I could see the tiredness in her pretty eyes. I hadn't let her get much rest the night before, and she'd been nonstop busy all day.

"I'm doing a shit job taking care of you already," I berated myself. "I swear, I'll do better, starting now."

"I wasn't aware it was your responsibility to take care of me," she murmured, a small smile lifting her lips. "But I like that you want the position."

"I don't want the position," I informed her as I lowered my head. This close, there was no way I could miss the hurt that flashed across her beautiful face. Skimming my lips over hers, I told her, "It's already mine—*you* are mine, Arella."

Her eyes lit up, and she stabbed her fingers into the back of my hair, pulling me closer. "That means you're mine, too."

"Always, baby."

--

Arella fell asleep on the drive home. After parking in my usual spot, I carefully lifted her out of the car and carried her to the elevators. On the ride up to my floor, she started to awaken, but I kissed her brow and softly told her to go back to sleep.

Inside my apartment, I placed her in our bed and tucked the covers around her. I ached to crawl in beside her and just hold her while she rested, but I had things that needed my attention.

Closing the bedroom door behind me, I walked into the kitchen, the farthest room from where Arella was sleeping, and called Mia. She'd responded to my earlier text by telling me to call her whenever I got the chance, and the sooner I got her on board with my plan, the better.

"Hey," she greeted before the first ring finished. "What's up?"

I didn't waste time with small talk but got straight to the point. I told her everything I knew about Arella's stalker, how she didn't want her parents to stress over her possibly being in danger, but after what happened earlier, it was apparent that she very much was in danger.

"Holy shit," Mia whispered. "Poor Arella, having to deal with all this crap without confiding in any of us." She sighed heavily. "I get her being concerned about stressing out Uncle Drake. With how sick he was before his liver transplant, we all tend to walk on eggshells around him with serious stuff."

"She needs security, though, Mia. But I know she's going to be stubborn about it." I scrubbed my free hand over my face in frustration. "She told the detective she would think about it, but I could tell from the look on her face that she wasn't taking him seriously enough."

"Yeah, that sounds just like her," she muttered. "Okay, let me talk to Barrick about this. I'm sure he'll have a suggestion or two on how to handle her."

"Thanks, Mia," I told her, a small measure of relief taking some of the tension out of my shoulders. "Call me back after you speak to him."

"Will do, my friend."

I got a text and ended the call so I could deal with it. Seeing it was my mother, I sent a quick reply. After checking the clock, I decided there was plenty of time to take a nap with the angel asleep in our bed.

Stripping down to my boxer briefs, I climbed in behind her.

"Mm," she sighed, turned over, and threw her arm around me. "Missed you."

I kissed the top of her head and rolled onto my back, taking her with me. She stretched out on me, pillowing her head on my chest, and cuddled closer. Within seconds, she was deeply asleep once again, making me smile. It wasn't long before I followed her into dreamland.

The feel of wet, hot suction on my cock had my eyes shooting open. I caught hold of Arella's ponytail, wrapping it around my wrist as I looked down at her sucking me off. "Baby," I groaned. "Fuck, that feels so good."

Her giggle caused vibrations along my entire shaft, making my balls tighten as I threatened to spill down her throat. Her silky-soft hands were stroking what she couldn't fit into her mouth, her wrist twisting up and down, pumping a rope of come from me.

She moaned it splashed onto her tongue, as if it were her favorite taste in the world. I knew if she kept making noises like that I wasn't going to last, no matter how good the relief from the micro-orgasm was for me. It wasn't enough, though. I wanted to blow every drop inside her tight pussy.

Using my hold on her hair, I tugged her off me.

"No," she whined, her lips swollen from sucking my cock, pouting. "I wasn't done."

"Shh, baby," I soothed, pulling off her dress. "We have the rest of our lives for you to suck me off to your heart's content. But right now, I need inside you."

Her eyes brightened, and she fell back onto the pillows, her thighs opening for me invitingly. "Condom."

Swallowing a curse because I kept forgetting, I opened the drawer beside the bed and grabbed the last condom. After all the times I'd fucked her the night before, I'd blown through the small stash I'd had in there. Not that it had mattered. We'd been so rough and they were so old, the damn things had broken more often than actually offered any real protection.

I sheathed my cock then sank balls deep inside her tight heat. The pleasure was so intense, we both groaned as I made us one. She was so wet and primed for me, telling me she'd gotten worked up while she was sucking my cock, and within a dozen hard pumps, she was coming apart for me.

"That's it, baby," I praised, slowing my pace so I could take my time with her and savor all of her. Lowering my head, I sucked one of her ripe nipples into my mouth and was rewarded with the flutter of her pussy spasming yet again around my shaft. "Your pussy feels so good, Arella. I want to spend the rest of my life right here, kneeling at this altar, worshiping you with my cock."

"Jordan!" she screamed, her eyes rolling back in her head.

My girl loved it when I talked dirty to her. It got her off almost as much as the feel of my dick branding the inside of her pussy, rubbing over her ultrasensitive G-spot. When I felt her gush as she came again, I knew the condom had broken yet again, and I had to hide my triumphant grin in her neck.

Call me a fucked-up asshole, but I wanted to get her pregnant. Needed the world to see that she belonged to me as her belly grew round with my baby. Just as I was going to brand her with the ring I was going to put on her finger very, very soon.

SIXTEEN
ARELLA

Breathless, I clung to Jordan long after we were both spent from the hours-long fuck fest. From the way I was so sticky between my legs and it was leaking onto my thighs, I knew the condom had broken. Again. The night before, after the third one had broken, Jordan had told me his stash was several years old.

His confession that he hadn't had sex in this apartment had made me so happy that it didn't even matter to me that I was overflowing with his come. He hadn't seemed all that concerned either, so I didn't freak out that it was very likely the best possible time for me to get pregnant.

I would only admit it to myself, but I'd been thinking of babies since before I turned eighteen. Of course, those babies were part of the fantasy I'd built in my head at the time, of a life with Jordan much like the one my sister had with Braxton. Jordan had effectively shattered those fantasies, however, and even though we were currently sleeping together, I didn't allow myself to imagine for even a minute that I could have that life with him now.

But even when things did end between us, maybe I

would have a little piece of that life after all. In the form of a baby we'd created together.

Pushing those thoughts away, I lifted my head to look down at him. He was on his back, where he'd finally fallen, completely exhausted, only minutes before. He'd dragged me on top of him, and I'd nearly fallen back asleep from the way he was rubbing his fingertips up and down my spine. But my stomach growled, reminding me that we hadn't eaten lunch earlier. A glance at the digital clock on the bedside table told me it was getting close to dinnertime, and I was about to venture into hangry territory if we weren't careful.

Jordan turned his head, following my gaze. Seeing the time, he muttered a curse and sat up. "Take a shower, baby. We'll go out for dinner."

"But I just wanted to veg in bed with you for the rest of the night. Can't we order in?" I pouted up at him when he climbed out of bed. "Jordan!" He picked me up with a grin and carried me into the bathroom. "I don't want to go out."

"We'll go somewhere small," he said, setting me on the sink and moving to turn on the shower. "I promise you'll enjoy the food, and we won't be gone long." When he walked back to me, I happily spread my legs to give him easy access to my naked body. But after a brief kiss, he stepped away. "You shower and get ready while I make a quick call."

As he walked out of the bathroom, I stuck out my tongue at him.

"I saw that, minx," he grumbled as he closed the door behind himself.

Giggling, I hopped down and crossed to the now-steaming shower. An hour later, I walked into the living room to find him already dressed and ready to go. He was wearing a suit, so I was glad I'd gone with the little black dress I'd packed, as well as taken the time to do my hair and makeup.

When his eyes landed on me, they darkened with hunger, and I watched as his jaw clenched. "Dinner and then I'm bringing you back here and fucking you all damn night," he said, almost as if he were warning me.

I picked up my purse and phone. "Don't threaten me with a good time." Winking at him, I walked to the door, calling over my shoulder, "But we need to stop at the drugstore on the way back and pick up condoms."

"Right," he muttered, following me out of his apartment. "Don't want to forget the protection. I've only filled you to your eyeballs with come in the last twenty-four hours."

I hid my smile as I pressed the call button for the elevator. It sounded like he was pouting, but I didn't look at him to confirm if he was or not, afraid he would see how much I liked that he was sulking over the idea of having to glove up with something we knew wouldn't break the next time he was inside me.

The elevator doors opened, and I walked in, leaving him there to pout or to follow me. I heard him grumble something to himself a split second before he grabbed me around the waist and turned me to face him. After hitting the button for the garage, he backed me against the wall and kissed me senseless.

I didn't even notice when we stopped several times on the way down. It was only when he finally released me and I saw the others exiting ahead of us that I realized we hadn't been alone.

Jordan took my hand in one of his and lifted his other to brush his thumb over my kiss-swollen bottom lip.

"You're so beautiful, I lose my mind when I'm this close to you."

I sucked his thumb into my mouth, causing him to groan like he was in physical pain. That sound vibrating out of his chest made me feel oddly powerful. Releasing the digit with a wet *pop*, I moved toward his car. With his hand still holding mine, he was right beside me, and he opened the passenger door for me.

Once we were in traffic and stopped at a red light, he reached out and touched my necklace, pulling my eyes to him. He had a smug smile on his devilishly handsome face as he skimmed his thumb over the interlocked hearts with the diamond in the center connecting them. "I was wondering if I was ever going to see you wear this," he murmured. "I've been aching to see it around your graceful neck for almost two years."

I frowned. "What are you talking about?" I covered the hearts. "My parents gave me this for Christmas."

"No way." He shook his head, reaching out to turn the hearts over. Whatever he saw when he did had his jaw clenching. "No," he denied again. "I gave you this necklace for your eighteenth birthday. Only, the hearts were engraved..." He dropped the hearts and pulled back his hand, clenching his fingers into a tight fist. "Didn't my parents give you my present?"

Swallowing hard, I looked out the windshield. "The light is green," I told him, my heart aching.

I heard his whispered curse, and then we were moving forward again.

"Did they give you the present?" he gritted out after he'd driven several blocks.

"They did," I confirmed, keeping my gaze straight ahead.

"So, why have I never seen you wear it?" He grasped my hand, interlocking our fingers. "And why would your parents buy you a necklace you already have?"

"Probably because they didn't realize I supposedly already owned it," I told him honestly. "Neither did I."

His fingers squeezed mine, hard, before he realized what he was doing and eased his hold. "Why?"

Everything I'd felt the night of my eighteenth birthday, from the moment his parents had arrived at my parents' house until I'd sat on my bed, looking at pictures of Jordan in Italy with Letizia, swept through me. Needing some distance from him but unable to get it within the car, I pulled away from his hold and clasped my hands together in my lap.

My eighteenth birthday was a day I thought would be the beginning of my forever with Jordan.

Instead, it had been the day my heart had been irrevocably broken.

I'd stayed his friend since then. Gone on as if nothing had changed between us. Even put on a brave face for my family when they thought I might fall apart.

Slowly, I'd put myself back together, but there were still parts missing. Parts I knew I would never find again because they had been crushed into sand somewhere on my old bedroom floor.

"The present your parents gave me from you is still in my closet back at my parents' house." I inhaled slowly, willing my voice not to tremble even as I fought the sting of tears. "Unopened."

His foot stomped on the brake, causing the car to jerk abruptly to a stop for the next red light. After a few tense seconds of silence, I chanced a glance at him. He was staring out the window at the car in front of us, his hands clenched around the steering wheel so tight, the white of his knuckles glowed in the dimness of the car's interior. His jaw was so rigid, a muscle ticked in his cheek.

Jordan didn't speak, didn't even move until the light turned green once again, and he carefully eased on the gas to stay with the flow of traffic. He looked pissed, but I felt too raw from the emotional war going on within me over everything I'd felt that night to really care if he was mad at me.

SEVENTEEN

JORDAN

Days before Arella's eighteenth birthday, I'd shopped for hours for her gift. It had to be perfect. Something that would tell her what I was feeling without overwhelming her or scaring her off. But at the same time, I'd needed it to tell her everything I was too much of a chickenshit to say aloud.

In truth, I'd been scared out of my ass to tell her what was in my heart back then. She'd still been in high school, for fuck's sake. What if what I was feeling—what I thought she might have felt too—was really just an infatuation that burned out for her?

Which was why I'd bitched-out when my father had said he had an issue in Italy that needed personal attention. I'd hopped on one of our private jets and asked my parents to go to Arella's party in my place. Work got crazy, and time ran away from me. It was as if one minute, it was her birthday, and then I blinked, and it was months later.

When she started dating that Lyle loser around the time her grandfather died, I thought I'd been right. That her feelings were just as I'd feared, and she'd moved on. But I hadn't given up. I'd stayed in the background, calling her and keeping in touch like nothing was different, biding my time.

It wasn't until Christmas Eve and Aunt Gabs had opened my eyes to a few things that I realized maybe I'd fucked up somewhere along the way.

Now, with the revelation that she'd never even opened that damned present all those months ago, it was glaringly evident where exactly I'd made such a huge mistake.

It was a bitter pill to swallow, but now I could see all too clearly that I'd screwed up royally by not going to that party. By sending someone else to give her such an important gift. By not telling her myself exactly what she meant to me.

I had no one else to blame but myself; I could see that. It was my fault she'd dated other guys. That she'd given all her firsts to someone else.

That she didn't fucking know I loved her more than life itself.

It was apparent I didn't deserve any of those firsts, because I hadn't had the balls to take what I could finally see we'd both wanted back then.

Swallowing the knot that had filled my throat, I realized I needed to focus on our present and future. She was mine now, and I wasn't fucking letting her go. Ever.

As I pulled into the parking lot of the little restaurant where we were having dinner, I promised myself that I would make everything up to her.

Turning off the car, I grabbed her hand and brought it to my lips. "Sit right there. Don't move. Please?"

A frown pulled her brows together, but she nodded, remaining quiet as I got out of the car. Closing the door behind me, I sent a text to Mia, begging her to do me a favor without asking questions. Immediately, I got a text back, assuring me she had it handled.

Pocketing my phone, I walked around to Arella's door and opened it for her. She was still frowning as I helped her out.

"Are you...angry with me?" she finally asked when we just stood there looking at each other for a long moment.

My eyes continued to eat up the sight of her, wondering where we might be at this point in our relationship if I hadn't fucked up so abysmally. Would I already have my ring on her finger? Would she have already given birth to our first baby, maybe with our second on the way?

Fuck, it was driving me crazy just thinking about all the possibilities. Telling myself to let the past go, I gently grasped her chin between my thumb and index finger, tilting her head up so I could kiss her. "No," I choked out when I broke the kiss. "I'm not angry with you, baby. Just myself."

She wrapped her arms around my waist. The feel of her pressed up against me only reminded me that I'd wasted so much time. I needed to fix this now, tonight. Vowing that not another day would pass without her knowing exactly what she meant to me, I kissed her again and then guided her toward the restaurant entrance.

As I'd expected and called ahead to warn, we were late. The place was small, but it had some of the best food in the entire city. There were people waiting, but I knew our table was ready for us. Instead of pausing at the hostess's stand, I kept my hand on the small of Arella's back and ushered her to the back of the restaurant.

"Rude," she hissed to me as we passed at least a dozen people waiting for their tables. "We can't just walk in and pick an empty table. You're mega rich, but you still have to be considerate. And at a glance, this place doesn't have an empty table to spare."

I stopped and dropped another kiss on her lips, putting a halt to the scolding she was giving me. When I lifted my head, her fingers were clenched in my suit jacket. "I promise we have a table waiting on us," I assured her with a grin.

"Oh," she murmured a little breathlessly. "O-okay, then."

Despite the turmoil my emotions were still in, I found myself laughing wholeheartedly as I linked our fingers and tugged her to where my parents were already enjoying glasses of wine at our table.

When Arella spotted them, she stopped walking, causing me to drag her a few steps before I realized what had happened. Pausing, I turned to look down at her and found her glaring up at me accusingly. "We're having dinner with your mother?"

My brows lifted. "Why are you mad? After how important it seemed to you yesterday, I thought this would be a nice surprise."

"It is," she whispered, shifting restlessly in front of me, and it dawned on me that she was feeling vulnerable.

Realizing this was only one more fuckup on my part, I gave her hand a reassuring squeeze and urged her toward our table.

As we neared, my father stood, but to my surprise, so did my mother. She grabbed my father's arm that he readily offered for support so she didn't have to use her cane, and once she was steady, she gave my girl a beaming smile.

I cleared my throat, knowing I had to get this right. Fuck, from here on out, I had to get everything right. "Mom, I want to introduce you—"

"Oh, honey, I've known Arella since she—" she started to interrupt.

"—to the love of my life. My future wife and the mother of your grandchildren," I finished. The rightness of those words eased something tight in my throat, and I silently vowed to introduce her to everyone we met exactly like that until she really was my wife and the mother of my children.

Arella's gasp was like a slash to my heart, reminding me that I hadn't even told her I loved her yet. But my mom's smile only got brighter, if that was possible, and she turned to my girl, pulling her in for a tight hug.

"Again, that's not news to me," Mom said with a soft laugh as she pulled back enough to wink down at Arella. "Although I was beginning to wonder if my son would ever get his head out of his ass and make things official with you."

Arella choked out a laugh, shooting me a teasing glare. "He does tend to keep it stuck pretty far up there, doesn't he?"

"Sadly, he's just like his father when it comes to things like this." My mom shook her head in mock despair. "But fortunately for us, they eventually realize their mistakes and work hard to fix them."

The two most important women in my life stood there, arms still around each other, and I'd never seen a sight that had warmed my heart so completely in my entire life. I didn't even care that they were making fun of me. It was well deserved, and I would happily let them continue for the rest of my life if only I got endless moments like this one.

"Ladies, if you are done being disappointed in my son and me," Dad muttered, his eyes seeming just as transfixed on the sight of them together as I was. "Maybe we could sit and have our first family dinner?"

EIGHTEEN
ARELLA

"Love of my life."

Those four words kept replaying in my head throughout dinner, making me so damn thankful that I was such a good actress because I was able to pretend like I was paying attention to at least half of the things Alexis Moreitti said to me. But, fuck, it was hard when her son had rocked my world repeatedly that evening.

The whole "my future wife and the mother of your grandchildren" didn't really even register for me. I'd heard it, but my brain hadn't fully computed it because all I could think about was that Jordan had just said I was the love of his life.

Pop-Pop had always told my siblings and me that the way a man introduced a woman to his mother was how he truly thought of her. That was why I'd always been kind of hung up on not sleeping with a guy until I met his mother. If he didn't at least introduce me as his girlfriend, then I didn't mean enough to him to give him my body.

I'd broken that rule for Jordan, but he'd more than made up for it with the way he'd introduced me to his mom.

One of my many fantasies had come true with how Alexis had welcomed me with open arms. After everything that had happened since my eighteenth birthday, I'd never thought it would happen. Hell, I'd thought she didn't even really like me. So many times, I'd caught her frowning at me. I'd always thought she was sizing me up and finding me lacking. That she didn't want me to be with her only son, but she was just too nice to tell me to stay away from him.

"I've never been one to spank my child," Alexis commented over dessert as she finished her glass of wine. Her eyes kept going from me to Jordan, and she shook her head as a small smile teased at her lips. "But over the past few years, there were times I seriously contemplated beating some sense into him. I mean, I could see how he felt about you." Reaching across the table, she took my hand, giving it a loving squeeze. "And I could see that you cared just as strongly. But Jordan was doing nothing but making mistake after mistake. I wanted to shake him and tell him to open his eyes, to stop breaking your heart, but I'd promised myself when he was younger that I would never interfere with his life."

Everything fell into place so suddenly, I almost laughed. "I honestly thought you hated me and didn't want me to be with him. That maybe you wanted...better for him."

I felt everyone at the table tense, but I wasn't brave enough to look at anyone but Alexis.

"Better?" she got out in a strangled voice. "Arella, sweetheart, do *you* not think you're good enough for Jordan? Because to me, there is no one better than you, sweet girl. From the first time Jordan mentioned your name when you were only sixteen, I knew you already held my son's heart in the palm of your hand. I always knew it was you who was going to be my daughter-in-law. Always."

My chin started to tremble, and I quickly bit my bottom lip to stop it. Shifting my gaze, I picked up my water glass and took a small sip, willing my tears not to spill over.

A rasped curse came from beside me. In the next moment, Jordan was on his feet and I was lifted into his arms. "Mom, I'll call you tomorrow," he said. "I have a few things to clear up before I lose my mind."

The sensation of eyes on me had me burying my face in Jordan's neck. Hidden away, the threat of tears only heightened, and I felt the embarrassing wetness on my cheeks. Vaguely, I heard his parents replying and then felt Jordan walking away.

I could picture people with their phones out taking pictures of us as we left, and I figured we would be all over entertainment news within the hour.

The chilly night air caused me to shiver as he stepped outside and walked toward his parked car. I felt his lips against my ear, and I tightened my arms around his shoulders. "Baby," he groaned as if he were in agony. "Please don't cry. I have so many things to tell you. Just hold on until we get home, and then I'll make it all better. I promise."

"I-I'm s-sorry I ruined d-dinner," I sobbed.

"Shh, baby, shh. No. You didn't ruin anything." He kept kissing my temple, my cheek, my hair. "I should have told you how much you mean to me—*how much I fucking love you*—years ago. But I was scared..." His exhale sounded pained, and I lifted my head to see tears glittering in his eyes.

Feeling as if I were in a dream, I touched my fingertips to his eyelashes. The dampness made me realize this was, in fact, reality. "I'm so sorry, Arella. Baby, please forgive me."

"Forgive you for what?" I asked, confused.

He'd reached his car. Carefully, he shifted me so he could open the door, then set me in the passenger seat. Once I was settled, he pulled the seat belt across me and snapped it into place before taking hold of both of my hands and bringing them to his mouth.

"I'm going to tell you everything as soon as we get home," he promised, kissing my palms. "But right now, I need you to know that what my mother just said is one hundred percent the truth. There is no one better for me than you. No other girl could ever touch my heart the way you do. No one could possibly give my life more meaning, more joy, more love than you. Even when you were sixteen and I was trying to tell myself and everyone else that we were just friends, I knew it was the biggest lie I'd ever spoken in my life. You are the other half of my soul. I've loved you for so long, I honestly can't remember a time when I didn't love you."

"Jordan." I couldn't blink my eyes fast enough to keep the tears at bay. As they spilled over, he cursed savagely and released my hand so he could gently wipe them away. "I-I love you too. I always have."

His hands on my face, there was no mistaking the way his entire body quaked at my words. "Babe, I've ached to hear you say that to me."

My laugh came out a little choked. "I could say the same about hearing you say it."

His kiss stole my breath along with my ability to think about anything but his taste on my tongue. I stabbed my fingers through his hair, clinging to him as I kissed him back like my very life depended on it. I wanted closer, wanted to feel every inch of his skin against my own. After hearing the words I'd been so desperate to hear for years, I needed him to show me just how true they were.

The sound of high-pitched laughter in the distance made me jerk in reaction as I was reminded that we were in a very public place. As badly as I wanted to feel Jordan inside me right that moment, I didn't want to have to explain to my parents why I'd been arrested for indecent exposure while having sex in my boyfriend's car outside the restaurant where I'd just had dinner with his mother and father.

Panting, Jordan lifted his head. "We need to get home before I do something that gets us both in trouble." He kissed the tip of my nose and straightened. With a wink, he closed the door then jogged around to the driver's side. Within a matter of moments, we were on the road, driving in the direction of his apartment.

As he drove, I couldn't tear my gaze from his profile. With the way he glanced my way every few seconds, I figured he was having the same problem but had to force his attention on the road so we could get home safely. Neither of us spoke until he pulled into his parking spot in the garage.

"Let me get your door," was all he said before he was rushing to get out and come around to my side.

Placing my hand in his, I stood and then threw my arms around his neck once again. "I need you," I breathed close to his ear. "Please hurry."

Clasping hands, we took off running for the elevator. Thankfully, no one else was waiting, and once we were inside, Jordan swiped a card and punched in a code, bypassing every other floor and sending us straight to his to avoid any delays of other people getting on or off.

No sooner had the elevator started to ascend than he was backing me against the rear wall and kissing me senseless. Clutching at his shoulders, I jumped and locked my legs around his back. My skirt lifted several inches, and I could feel cool air on my ass as my thong was exposed. Jordan skimmed his fingers up the outsides of my thighs before gripping my ass with both hands while his hips thrust against me, promising me without words that he was going to give my body everything it ached for.

Vaguely, I heard the ding of the elevator doors opening, and then Jordan was carrying me to his apartment. It took a few tries to get the door open because he didn't want to stop kissing me long enough to see what he was doing. Once we were inside, he kicked the door closed and then pressed me up against it. My thong was shifted to the side, and then three large fingers were thrust into my core.

"So wet for me," he groaned. "Such a needy little pussy. Do you think I can make it purr for me, baby?"

"Jordan, don't tease me," I pleaded. "I need you."

Cursing, he pulled back just enough to unfasten his belt and slacks. I had to ease the hold my legs had on his waist so he could pull his cock free, but within seconds, he was filling me the way I craved.

"Already clenching around me," he groaned. "And without a condom again. Do you want me to fill you with my come, Arella? Do you want me to put a baby inside you?"

"Yes," I sobbed, already close to a powerful release. "I want it all. You, us, a baby. Please, Jordan. Give me everything I've ever wanted."

"I'm going to," he promised, his lips latching on to my neck. "I'm going to make every dream you have come true. Just say the word, and it's yours, love."

"Tell me you love me again," I cried. "Please. I-I want to hear the words as I come."

I felt him grow thicker inside me and knew he was just

as close as I was. As he lifted his head, our eyes locked, and he swallowed roughly before whispering the words I'd never thought I would ever hear from him. "I love you so fucking much, baby. I always have."

"I love you too," I moaned, my pussy gushing around his girth as his hips pounded against me.

"Arella," he choked out my name as I watched his face twist as if in utter agony. "Baby, I can't hold back."

My legs tightened around his hips. "I don't want you to. Give me everything you have, Jordan. I need it."

"Fuck, fuck, fuck," he chanted as he stepped away from the door and dropped to his knees right there on the floor. I squealed, but his arms held me close to him, protecting me from any impact. But then he was drilling me into the floor as if he couldn't get deep enough inside me. "How many gallons do you think I've already emptied into you?" he rasped at my ear as he increased his pace even more. "How many more do you think it will take until you start to swell with our baby?"

The pleasure was so intense, I couldn't even answer him. But he didn't seem to care. I loved that he seemed so determined to get me pregnant. Earlier that evening, I'd thought once we were over, at least I would have a part of him to hold on to. But now, I couldn't wait to give him all the babies he wanted, to raise them together, and to have the life I'd dreamed about for so damn long.

"As soon as I can breathe again, I'm going to take you to bed and do this over and over again," he vowed. "You're going to get sick of my touch."

Unable to speak, I could only shake my head adamantly. Never. I was never going to get sick of his touch. I ached for it every minute of the day. Even when he was right beside me, I craved him to the point of madness.

"No?" He grinned like a predator, and the thought that I was his prey only made me clench around him tighter. "You sure about that, babe? You're mine now."

"You...say that like...it's a bad thing," I panted.

"I've held back for so long. What I feel for you, it's become an obsession. Now that you've said you love me, I can't contain it any longer. I am never going to let you go." His head fell back on his shoulders, the muscles in his neck straining as he shouted my name, and I felt him come deep inside me.

The feel of his hot release shot me over the edge, and my pussy locked down on his cock, my walls contracting around his shaft and milking every last drop out of him as I whimpered my way through the strongest orgasm of my life.

NINETEEN
JORDAN

She loves me.

That was all I could think as I found the strength to stand and lift her into my arms. Carrying her into our bedroom, I placed her carefully on the bed before going into the bathroom to get a damp washcloth and towel to clean her up.

When I returned, she was already half asleep, her eyes barely open as she watched me with a contented smile on her kiss-swollen lips. I wiped up the mess coating her thighs and then stripped off the rest of her clothes. Once she was naked, I tucked the covers around her before taking the washcloth and towel back into the bathroom. Dropping them into the hamper, I finished removing my own clothes on my way back to her.

An adorable soft snore reached my ears before I even returned. Stopping beside my side of the bed, I looked down at her.

She loves me.

Everything I'd spent so long trying to contain was free now. There was no holding back the obsessive, possessive part of myself that needed to be her everything. Just as she was mine.

Pulling the covers back, I slid in bed and pulled her against me. She snuggled against me, her hand resting right over my heart as she pillowed her head on my chest. I covered her hand with my own and dropped the other to caress my fingertips over one of her hips. She sighed happily and squirmed even closer, tossing one of her legs over both of mine until she was lying half on top of me.

"Sleep," I said, kissing the top of her head.

"'Kay," she murmured, and I felt her lips touching the skin of my chest. "Love you."

"I love you, baby."

Soon she was lightly snoring again, and I let the sound lure me to sleep as well.

The next time I opened my eyes, sunlight was pouring through the window, and my home phone was ringing. The cordless extension in my bedroom had never sounded more annoying than it did right then. Groaning, I reached out to grab the noisy thing, but Arella grumbled unhappily and tried to cling to me.

"Let it ring," she slurred sleepily. "It will stop eventually." As if on cue, the phone stopped, and I felt her smile against my skin. "See? Told you."

"Mm," I agreed, closing my eyes again. Sleep tried to take me under again…

And then the phone started ringing again. Arella whined, her smile turning into a pout. "Who even has a landline these days? I changed my mind. Make it stop."

"Motherfuck," I growled, wishing whoever was on the other end of that call to the deepest bowels of hell. "When we buy a house, we won't get a landline, I swear." Picking up the cordless, I turned it to silent and then threw it across the room.

The clang of it shattering as it hit the wall made Arella giggle, and I rolled her onto her back. After kissing her, I pillowed my head on her chest and closed my eyes again. Sleep was fading quickly, my cock forcing me to wake up fast, but I needed to talk to her before I put my dick in her again.

She combed her fingers through my hair, scratching my scalp with her nails. Nothing outside of sex with her had ever felt so good.

The doorbell ringing echoed through the entire apartment, causing her to pause her coma-inducing scratches.

"Maybe it's whoever was trying to call earlier?" she suggested.

Muttering curses under my breath, I pushed up onto all fours over her. Fuck, she was so beautiful with her hair all tousled and her eye makeup smeared under her eyes. I could have stayed like that all day, just staring down at her and soaking up the sight of her relaxing in our bed.

But then the doorbell rang again, reminding me that the outside world was trying its damnedest to intrude. Lowering my head, I kissed her quickly before jumping out of bed. Grabbing a pair of basketball shorts out of my dresser, I pulled them on and stomped unhappily to the front door.

When I jerked the door open, Mia squeaked in surprise. "Gods, warn a person!" she scolded. "I swear, I thought you might have been dead when you didn't answer your cell or the landline."

I scrubbed a hand over my face, grunting at the feel of the stubble on my jaw. I needed to shave before I chafed Arella's skin, but all I wanted was to crawl back into bed with her and continue just lying on top of her while she scratched my head.

"What do you want, Mia?" I groused.

"Excuse you, Moreitti," she snipped and pushed something against my chest

I dropped my hand in time to catch the small box wrapped in metallic red gift paper. Seeing the unopened present, I remembered the favor I'd asked of my best friend the night before.

"No one was home when I stopped by Uncle Drake's house last night, so I had to wait and get it this morning." Her green eyes skimmed over me dispassionately. "By the looks of you, I doubt you minded the delay. You're welcome, by the way." She *hmphed* and turned away.

"Thank you," I called after her belatedly. "I owe you one, Mia."

"You're damn right, you do." The elevator doors opened, and she flipped me off as she stepped into it. "By the way, you look like you got into a fight with a wildcat. Apparently, the cat won."

Confused, I glanced down at myself, wondering what she was talking about, only to find scratches and a few bite marks on my chest, arms, and shoulders. The sight of how passionate Arella was only made my cock harden, tenting my shorts. Closing the door, I turned to go back to the bedroom.

Arella was sitting up in the center of the bed when I walked in. The covers were pulled to her chest, and her glossy dark hair had been finger-combed and pulled over her shoulder. The sight of her stole my breath, and I just stood at the end of the bed, looking down at the angel that was all mine.

She loves me.

Her blue-gray gaze fell on the present in my hand, and I saw her stiffen. "Where did you get that?"

I tightened my fingers around it, but I didn't take my eyes off her. "Don't be angry."

Her brow furrowed, but after a brief hesitation, she gave a firm nod. "Okay."

"I asked Mia to pick up the present my parents delivered on your eighteenth birthday."

Arella sat up a little straighter, her arms crossing over her chest in a protective, guarded kind of way that made me ache to have the soft, cuddly version of my girl back.

"That was at my parents' house," she muttered.

"Mia made up an excuse that she needed to pick up something from your old room." I sat on the end of the bed, turning so we were facing each other. Placing the present between us, I left it there as I watched her cautiously. "She tried to get it last night, but no one was home. So she had to wait until this morning."

Her eyes dropped to the pretty metallic red wrapping before quickly looking away. "Why does it matter so much? It's just a present."

"If it's just a present, why didn't you open it?" I asked, trying and failing to keep the rasp of emotion out of my voice.

She lifted one bare shoulder. "I just didn't."

"But you kept it. Didn't stomp on it or throw it away." I touched my index finger to the matching red ribbon. It was still perfectly wrapped, even though it was over eighteen months later.

"It was from you. I might have been too upset and hurt to open the damned thing, but I couldn't bring myself to destroy it or even toss it out."

I nodded in understanding. "When you never

mentioned the present, I just thought maybe you didn't want to hurt my feelings or ruin the friendship we had. I had no idea you hadn't even opened it."

"Jordan, the only thing I wanted for that birthday was you. And then you bailed, sent your parents and that stupid present." She nudged the box with her foot, pushing it closer to me and farther away from herself. "Then..." She swallowed roughly and started again. "And then I saw you all over social media with Letizia. You were leaving some nightclub in Italy. You had her lipstick all over you, and then someone tweeted that they saw you going into her place..."

"Open it," I commanded when I heard the hitch in her voice.

Her gaze snapped to mine, and I saw hurt flashing out of those blue-gray depths. "I don't want to."

"Please," I rasped out. "For me, love. I need you to open it."

"No," she argued mutinously. "If it was so important to you for me to see what was inside, you should have given it to me yourself in the first place."

"You're right," I agreed. Taking a deep breath, I went for broke and started from the very beginning. "Nevaeh's eighteenth birthday was a life-changing night for me. I know it was a hard time for you and your family, with your dad so sick, but I'll always remember that night because it was the moment my heart felt like it finally started to beat."

My eyes caressed over her lovingly as I remembered that party. Everyone standing around trying to put on a brave face for Nevaeh but failing because Drake was so sick, they didn't know if it was the last birthday party he would ever share with his children. I'd been talking to Mia and Barrick, flirting with Nevaeh to piss off Braxton and distract myself from the utter boredom—and loneliness—that seemed to be my constant companion.

Then I'd heard this sweet, bell-like giggle, and something inside me had lit up. I'd glanced around, looking for the source of the sound that had made me able to actually feel my heart beating in my chest for the first time. When my eyes fell on Arella, I hadn't even recognized her for a moment. It had been years since I'd seen her. With Mia living in Virginia at the time, I was rarely in California, and when I was, it was only to visit with my parents.

There she'd stood, with her dark hair flowing down her back in soft waves, wearing a red dress that clung to her perfect curves. I'd taken two steps toward her before I even realized what I was doing when Mia grabbed my arm and dug her nails in my arm. "You realize she's only sixteen, right?"

"Who?" I'd muttered, annoyed that she was keeping me from my destiny.

"Arella," she'd hissed. I reluctantly tore my gaze away from my angel and looked down at Mia, still not completely understanding what she was trying to tell me. "The girl you were about to grab and probably disappear with, that's Arella. And you should really remember that she is sixteen."

"That goddess is only sixteen?" I choked out as I turned my head back to run my eyes longingly over the beauty standing in a group of her cousins. Her smile lit up the whole room, her musical laugh pulling every gaze to her, and even though I knew the majority of the people in the room were related to her in some way, I wanted to hide her away so no one but I could have the privilege of seeing and hearing all that sweetness.

Mia grabbed my chin and jerked my head back to look at her. "Read my lips, Jordan. Sixteen. S-I-X-T-E-E-N."

Jerking my face out of her hold, I stepped back from her. "Yeah, fuck. Okay. I get it." I turned my back on Arella just as she started to look in my direction, telling myself that Mia was right. The girl was too young.

I locked down what I was feeling, told myself to stay far, far away from her, and focused on torturing Braxton and even Barrick a little.

Only, it didn't work. I couldn't help looking over at Arella every few minutes. Each time I did, I would catch her looking right back, curiosity shining out of those eyes, the blue-gray my new favorite color.

Blinking away the memories, I grasped Arella's hand and tugged. She came willingly, and I pulled her naked body into my lap. Cupping her face in one hand, I kissed the tip of her nose then her lips. "I fell for you that night, baby. I fell so hard and so deep that I didn't know which way was up. I told myself that we could only ever be friends, and I was okay with that. As long as I got a fix of you every now and then, I could survive without you. I threw myself into work, tried to fuck you out of my system with other women..." She flinched, and I kissed her again. "And every time I fucked them, I would feel physically sick afterward until I eventually gave up trying to work you out of my system. But I kept telling myself that I was okay with us just being friends."

"I'm not sure I want to hear all of this," she muttered unhappily.

"I'm not sure I want to tell you all of it, but I don't want there to be any more misunderstandings between us." I pressed my forehead to hers. "I told myself and anyone who even so much as breathed your name in my presence that we were only friends, but the lock I'd put on my feelings for you was starting to crumble. The closer your eighteenth birthday got, the more I could feel it breaking away, and it scared me. I knew if I let go and showed you how much I loved you, how much I wanted you, it would scare you away. I was worried it would make you run from me, and I didn't know if I could survive that."

"Never," she said with an adamant shake of her head. "I would never run from your love for me."

"You haven't seen the full extent of how much I want and need you yet, Arella. It might scare you." I glanced down at the present and picked it up. "I wanted to buy you a ring, but I figured your dad would have killed me if I'd asked to marry you while you were still in high school. And I still didn't know if what I was hoping you felt for me was as strong as what I was feeling. My biggest fear was that it was just an infatuation and you would eventually get bored with me and move on."

TWENTY
JORDAN

"If you had shown up at my party with a ring, I would have married you that night," she confessed, blowing my mind. "It wouldn't have mattered to me if my dad didn't like it. I wouldn't have cared that I was still in high school. All I have ever wanted was to be yours and for you to be mine."

"I realize that now." Placing the present in her hand, I wrapped her fingers around it. "I'm so sorry I wasted so much time. If I hadn't been such a pussy about your feelings for me fading, or of scaring you off, then we could have been together this entire time."

The beginnings of a smile teased at her lips. "Jordan, you seem so worried about me being scared of your feelings, but I don't think you truly understand my own. I'm just as possessive of you as you say you are of me." The ghost smile disappeared, and her gaze hardened. "And I can promise you, if you cheat on me or I see any other woman who isn't related to you or me within two feet of you, I will destroy you both."

A relieved laugh escaped me. "Baby, you will never

have to worry about that. I swear on everything I love, I am yours. Now and always." Kissing her to seal the vow, I tucked her closer and lifted my head. "Please open your present."

She huffed like it was the biggest inconvenience of her life, but I saw the glitter in her eyes. Taking her time, she lifted one edge of the wrapping paper. I sat there holding her as she finally unveiled the jewelry box and lifted the lid.

When she looked down at the necklace, her free hand touched the one that was still around her neck. "It really is the same," she murmured.

"Not quite." I took the box and pulled out the necklace. Laying the charm in my palm, I turned over the double hearts to show the inscription I'd had added.

Now and always, our hearts are one.

I watched as she read the words. Her chin began to tremble, and tears spilled over her lashes as she lifted her gaze to mine. "Jordan," she sobbed. "You... Damn it, I should have opened this that night."

"No," I told her, wiping away one of her tears. "I should have given it to you personally." Reaching around her, I unhooked the necklace her parents gave her for Christmas and placed it in the now-empty jewelry box. "You can pass this one on to one of our daughters. But this one..." I placed the one I'd bought around her neck and fastened the clasp. "I want to see it around your neck often, love."

As it fell into place, she touched her fingertips to the double hearts, her thumb rubbing over the diamond that held them together. "I don't ever want to take it off."

I trailed my fingers down her neck to the valley between her breasts. "I haven't had sex with anyone but you in over two years," I confessed. "And I've never touched Letizia. She's drunkenly tried to seduce me, and the international tabloids have hyped it up that we were together. But I swear it was all lies. The only relationship I ever had with her was as her babysitter. My dad figured since I had so much experience in the past with being a spoiled and overprivileged brat, I should keep some of his friends' and clients' kids out of trouble too."

Arella pressed her hands against my chest, pushing me onto my back. She came down over me, a sad smile on her face. "Promise me that no matter what, from now on, we tell each other everything that is on our minds. So much pain and heartache could have been avoided if we'd just talked openly to each other this entire time. We both made so many assumptions that weren't even close to reality."

"I promise." Tucking a few locks of hair behind her ear, I let my fingers trail over her shoulder and down her back. "Now tell me when we can go house hunting and start planning the wedding."

Her eyes widened for a moment before she rolled them. "The wedding planning usually happens after a proposal, Moreitti."

"I have to ask your dad first."

Her eyes darkened. "Um, yeah, about that..."

I tensed. "What?"

"Daddy kind of... Well, he isn't your biggest fan at the moment, babe." She sighed. "After my birthday party, he told me to give you a little while. That sometimes guys take a little longer to pull their heads out of their asses. But then you didn't show up again until Pop-Pop died. By then, Daddy had been the one to push me to move on and even introduced me to Lyle..."

No wonder Drake had been so cold toward me at the funeral. He'd told his daughter to hold out hope, and I'd been too focused on work and trying not to think about Arella. I'd let them both down. Fuck.

"But he knew Lyle was just a rebound. Just like—"

I covered her mouth with my hand. "Please don't put the names of the guys you've fucked in my head, love. Unless you really do want me to start a hit list, just keep that shit to yourself."

She kissed my palm before pulling my hand away, the grin on her face sheepish. "Sorry."

"I'll still talk to your dad. I want to do everything right from here on out. Including getting his blessing to marry you." I stroked her cheek. "Until then, can we please go house hunting? As much come as I've filled you with in the last few days, we need to get a bigger place sooner rather than later for all the babies I'm going to fuck into you."

She licked her lips, squirming over my already steel-hard cock. "H-how many babies are we talking about?" she asked breathlessly, opening her legs.

I could feel how wet she was already and moved to flip her under me, only to have to force myself to keep from thrusting into her when she wrapped her legs around my hips. "Fuck," I groaned. "I need to ask you something. And I need an answer soon, love. Because if you're already pregnant, there is no way in hell I'm letting you do any stunts for the damn thing."

"Stunts?" she repeated. "I've never actually done any stunts before. Is this about that part you were talking about yesterday?"

"Yeah." It was hard to think when she was completely naked beneath me with my necklace glittering up at me in the sunlight shining through the window. All that separated my throbbing cock from her soaked pussy was the thin material of my basketball shorts. "I might possibly put some money into a new movie franchise if you're willing to be the lead."

Her eyes filled with curiosity, and I told her all the key points of the plot line. Her interest only heightened, and I could actually feel her excitement bubbling up. But then I had to tell her about her uncle. "Garon Steel is the one who approached me about investing. He will be the other executive producer on the project."

"No," she said, already shaking her head. But I could also see the disappointment on her face. She wanted this; she just didn't want to have to work with Garon. "I can't, Jordan. If it were anyone else, I would have already said yes. But not him. He's evil."

"How so?"

Her lips twisted into a grim line before she pushed at my chest. I sat up, and she pulled the covers over her as she sat facing me. "This isn't public knowledge, but when I was a baby, he tried to sue my mom. The production company he had at the time was going bankrupt, and he needed some fast cash. He tried to scare her into paying him hush money to keep him from dragging her through the tabloid trash. Mom's birth ended Pop-Pop's marriage to Garon's mother. Claudia Steel ended up with most of Cole's money at the time because Mom's very existence proved he'd cheated on his wife."

Anger at the man for trying to exploit money out of people I considered my own family made me see red. "Did she pay?"

"Of course not." She sighed. "Pop-Pop stood behind her, got her a lawyer, and showed Garon which of his two children he was supporting in the matter. But Garon still persisted. Daddy made a deal with him because he knew it was stressing Mom out. If Garon backed off and dropped the ridiculous lawsuit, Daddy would arrange for his next production to get the backing it needed by the right people. Obviously, it helped him, and that's how he became a part of Strive Studios."

"I didn't know anything about that, love. If I had, I never would have even taken the meeting with him."

She gave me a small smile. "I know. It's not something we talk about, and thankfully, it never made it to the tabloids. I didn't doubt your loyalty. Mom wasn't worried so much about herself back then, but Nevaeh and I were little, and she didn't want us to be dragged through that ugliness. Eventually, Mom let Pop-Pop publicly claim her as his daughter, but they did the story exclusively through Aunt Harper's magazine, *Rock America*, so they could control what was printed as much as possible."

Sadness filled her eyes, and I pulled her back onto my lap, needing to comfort her. After a moment, she spoke again. "Then when he died, it became a major entertainment story that she and us grandkids inherited everything even remotely associated with Cole Steel and the Steel Entrapment brand, while Garon didn't get a single cent. Garon tried to contest the will, but after a few months, he dropped his case."

Cuddling closer, she kissed my chin. "I want to do a project with you, Jordan. And I'm really interested in the part, but...I can't if Garon is going to be a part of it too. I won't betray my mom like that."

"No, baby. I won't ask that of you." If I'd known any of what Garon had put Lana through, I never would have replied back to the first email he'd sent me, let alone taken the meeting with him. "I'll tell Garon he's going to have to find someone else to help back this movie."

"But it could be a really profitable investment," she

argued. "Just because I won't do it doesn't mean you have to give it up too."

"I'll find a different movie to back," I told her with a shrug. "One we can do together." I carefully laid her back against the pillows, my hand flattening against her lower abdomen. "Preferably after this little one arrives."

Her hand covered mine as a dreamy look filled her eyes. "We don't even know if there is going to be a little one yet."

"When was your last period?"

She rolled her eyes. "I'm not refuting that it is a good time for me to get pregnant, just that we don't know if I am yet or not."

"How long until we *will* know?" I asked with a pout.

"I don't know. At least a few weeks."

"That's plenty of time for us to find a house." I gave her a long, deep kiss. When she started to cling to me, I hopped out of bed, causing her to whine unhappily. "You, my love, need to shower while I call a real estate agent."

"Fine," she grumbled petulantly. "But I'm going to want coffee."

"Better enjoy it now, baby. Because as soon as we find out if you're pregnant, it will be decaf for the next nine months," I warned, standing over her.

She shrugged. "I'm okay with that."

"While we're talking about things you're okay with..." I backed slowly toward the door. "I'm having Taylor find you your own personal assistant." Her eyes widened in surprise, and I continued. "Preferably an openly gay, male assistant."

"I'm okay with that too, but I don't think you can legally make that a requirement."

"I can't, but Taylor can keep interviewing until she finds what I'm looking for. One who is as efficient as she is, but who won't drool over my woman's ass and tits."

Arella grinned. "Taylor did like what she saw, huh?" Jealousy spiked in my veins, causing my nostrils to flare and her to giggle. "Go make the call so we can find our house, babe."

"I don't know." I took a step back toward the bed. "Maybe I want to remind myself who you belong to."

"If you get back in this bed, we won't be leaving it for the rest of the day," she threatened. "And then we will be one day closer to finding out if we're pregnant and one day short of finding our forever home."

Her logic stopped me from diving into bed. "Well played, love. Now get that sexy ass in the shower."

TWENTY-ONE
ARELLA

I DIDN'T THINK HOUSE HUNTING WOULD BE SO MUCH fun, but once we started looking at places, I realized how mistaken I was. At every property we were shown, I walked into each room and could actually picture how I would decorate it. But in the end, there would always be something that turned me off about the house, and I couldn't see us living there forever.

As we stepped outside of the latest listing our real estate agent had dropped everything to show us that afternoon, I felt a little sad that even after seeing seven other properties, none of them had been perfect. We'd seen two houses in the same neighborhood as his parents, three closer to my own, and a few in between. They had all been big enough to accommodate a growing family, but none of them had felt... like ours.

"I do have a place that just went on the market in Beverly Hills," Peter said as he handed over a printout of the house's details. "But if you want to see it, we have to do it now. This place is a hot spot and won't be available for long. Who the neighbors are alone will sell this place unseen."

"What do you think, baby?" Jordan asked, skimming the paper in my hand over my shoulder.

With over twenty-thousand square feet, the house had six bedrooms and nine baths. I wanted a big home, but did we really need *that* much house?

Then I saw the address and handed the paper back to the real estate agent. "No thank you."

Jordan frowned down at me. "You don't even want to see it?"

I shook my head. "We don't need that much space. Maybe we should give that place a mile from your mom's house a second look."

"You didn't like the HOA woman who came over while we were viewing the house," he reminded me. "If we bought that place and had to deal with her, you would murder her."

I smirked. "The neighbors would thank me and then probably help me hide her body."

Peter chuckled. "That has been a huge factor in everyone turning down that house. It's perfect until Nancy comes over and starts snipping at potential buyers."

I wondered if constantly being annoyed with Nancy was a better option than living at the Beverly Hills house. I mean, if Nancy did piss me off to the point I murdered her, would a jury really find me guilty once they knew the whole story?

Jordan pulled the paper out of Peter's hand. "Let's at least take a look," he argued. "It's in a great neighborhood, and Mia said the school district is good. It was why she picked—" He broke off when he saw the look on my face. Clenching his jaw, he turned to the real estate agent and shook his hand. "I'll let you know if we want to view this property."

"Let me know in the next few days. I seriously doubt it will be available by Monday." He offered me his hand, but when I lifted mine to shake it, Jordan stepped between us.

"I'll let you know," he said in a tight voice. Putting his hand on the small of my back, Jordan turned me toward the SUV waiting for us at the end of the driveway.

The driver was quick to open the back door for us, and Jordan helped me inside before climbing in beside me. As soon as we were moving, he hit the button to put up the partition between the driver and us and pulled me onto his lap.

I cuddled close, feeling tired after the hours of viewing house after house.

Jordan gently grasped my chin and tilted my head up so I was looking into his eyes. "Want to tell me why you're so against living in the same neighborhood as Mia?" he murmured.

"Not really." I pushed his hand away and started to lay my head back on his shoulder, but he wasn't going to allow me to avoid this particular conversation.

"Do you still think I have a thing for her?"

"I...don't know," I told him honestly.

His dark eyes softened. "The only woman I have ever been in love with is you, Arella. Mia and I have only ever been best friends. Nothing more."

"The best friend you had sex with," I reminded him in a voice tight with suppressed emotion.

Jordan released a heavy sigh. "Yeah, and I can honestly say it was probably the most awkward sex of my life." He brushed his lips over my ear, making me shiver. "I'm going to tell you about this, but then can we please never speak about it again?"

I shrugged, unable to give him a verbal answer when I wasn't sure I could make that promise.

Groaning, he tightened his arms around me. "Mia was in a dark place at the time. She'd just found out that the future she always had planned out wasn't going to happen. With her knee so fucked up, she couldn't dance professionally anymore, and it was breaking her. She came over to my house one night, and when I hugged her in an attempt to comfort, she kissed me. We were young and dumb, and things got out of hand. I'm not going to lie and say I didn't get off, because I did, but it took some serious effort to get there. Because it..." He muttered a curse, and I saw his face actually turn green. "It felt *wrong*. Even kissing her was weird. I love her, but I've never looked at her and felt anywhere close to what I feel for you, baby. We grew up together, and she feels like family to me. Then afterward, she regretted it just as much as I did, and she couldn't even look at me for the longest time. I was scared I'd lost my best friend."

Something uncoiled deep inside me. The release of pressure was so intense, I actually whimpered in relief and threw my arms around his neck as I attacked his mouth with my own.

Ever since I'd found out that Jordan and Mia had slept together, I'd felt like there was this weight sitting on my chest. It hadn't stopped me from loving my cousin, but it became difficult to look at her and not hurt when I thought about the guy to whom I'd given my heart.

Jordan groaned and cupped the back of my head, taking control of the kiss. Breathing hard, he turned me on his lap so I was straddling him, and I was thankful I'd worn a dress with a loose skirt. I'd never been so thankful for a partition before in my life. I needed him inside me, and I didn't even think the driver being able to see us would have stopped me right then.

Jordan's hands pulled the dress up to my waist and quickly pushed my thong out of his way as he stuffed three fingers into my pussy. Biting back a moan, I started working on his belt, needing him inside me. When he broke the kiss to help me, I was panting. "We... We can look at the house."

"Tomorrow," he growled, pulling his cock from his pants and thrusting roughly up into me. "I'm spending the rest of this day inside you."

Dropping my head to his shoulder, I sank my teeth into his neck right below his ear and whispered, "I'm okay with that plan."

I felt his shudder of pleasure along with a spurt of his come hitting my walls. Knowing I could make him come a little like that gave me a feeling of power, and I bounced faster on his cock.

His fingers bit into my ass, but he didn't try to slow my rhythm. "You have to know that I have only ever been in love with you," he rasped as he lowered his head to lick across my collarbone. "No one has ever possessed my heart but you, Arella. Only you, baby. Only ever you."

"Jordan," I whined, my inner walls clenching around him as I fought hard not to come. "It's always been you, too. No one else has come close to touching my heart but you."

"Thank fuck," he groaned. "Baby, I love you. Tell me you'll always be mine. Promise me you're only ever going to love me."

"Yes, yes, yes," I chanted before kissing him.

But he pulled back all too soon. "Say it," he

commanded, his jaw tight as if he were fighting to hold on just as badly as I was.

"I'm yours," I vowed and felt him thicken even more inside me, telling me he was close to releasing whether he wanted to or not. "I'll only ever love you."

He jerked my head down and buried his face in my chest, muffling his shout as he came so hard his entire body trembled. Feeling his thick, hot come flooding my pussy, I couldn't fight my own orgasm any longer. I rocked against him, prolonging the pleasure for both of us as we tried to catch our breath.

Sweat coated our skin, and I felt him licking my shoulder and neck. "You taste so fucking good," he rasped at my ear. "I'm taking you home and eating you for dinner."

Closing my eyes, I melted against him and closed my eyes. "Promises, promises."

TWENTY-TWO
JORDAN

The sound of my cell ringing pulled me from a deep sleep. Cracking open one eye, I glanced at the digital clock on the bedside table on my side of the bed and bit back a curse when I saw it was just after ten at night.

I sat up and reached for my phone before it could wake Arella. I'd worn her out all evening, only pausing long enough to feed her before we'd both fallen into an exhausted sleep less than an hour before.

Seeing it was Detective Kirtner, I quietly got to my feet and left the bedroom so I didn't disturb her. As I closed the door behind me, I answered. "Moreitti," I clipped out.

"Going to ask you a question, and I want you to be honest." His tone was matter-of-fact and possibly even a little accusatory.

I tensed at his tone but mentally reminded myself that this guy was a cop and was trying to help keep Arella safe. "I'm listening."

"Yesterday, did you and Miss Stevenson happen to do anything in her dressing room that might have been...intimate?"

"Why does that matter?" I gritted out.

"Because after the executives cleared out yesterday, I had a forensic team come in and sweep it just to be on the safe side. They found evidence that there might have been a hidden camera in the room. The camera itself was missing, but there was a piece of the device left behind."

My blood ran cold, and I dropped onto the couch in the living room in disbelief. "You've got to be kidding me."

"Wish I were. The remnants of the device suggested it was high-tech, very expensive, and not easy for the technologically challenged to install." Kirtner exhaled heavily. "So, I'm going to ask you again. Is it possible that you and Miss Stevenson may have been intimate in her dressing room? Because if you were, that would explain the violent way the place was destroyed. Seeing her with someone else, on top of her show ending, which has effectively taken away seeing her as part of his regular routine, could have caused him not only to escalate yesterday, but could also mean that she is in even more danger now."

"Not to mention there could now be a sex tape floating around out there," I muttered to myself, but I heard his curse.

"I'll take that as a yes, then. Hadn't considered the potential for that."

The thought of someone else watching me fuck Arella, their eyes on her as she was lost in the throes of passion as she came on my cock and then sucked me off, made me see red. And now that sick fuck could have already put it on porn sites and countless other places. The entire world could have been watching my woman being fucked right that moment.

"I have to go. I need to make sure she isn't all over the damn internet right now."

"I'd worry about yourself too, Mr. Moreitti."

"Who the fuck cares about me?" I snarled, and I disconnected the call before I started yelling at the man.

I didn't matter. It was Arella whom I couldn't stand being hurt over what we did in the privacy of her dressing room going viral. Any more than I could handle the thought of the population fucking their hands to the sexy sight of Arella's ripe ass and juicy pussy as she squirted all over my cock.

Calling Mia, I jumped to my feet and began to pace. When she picked up after the third ring, I didn't even give her time to speak. "Who is the person your mom calls when she needs to pull something off the web about one of her clients? Is it Mieke?"

"Um, hello to you too, Mr. Grumpy." I heard her yawn and realized I might have woken her up. It was only after ten, but she did have Emerson to deal with, and the little hellion was a handful, not to mention Mia was pregnant again. "What did you do that Mieke needs to have erased from the dreadful interweb?"

"Mia, just give me her number." When all I heard was tense silence on her end, I muttered a quick, "Please."

"Fine," she huffed. "But I want answers tomorrow. I'll text you her contact information, but she lives in Nashville. It's going to be after midnight her time."

"Noted," I bit out. Not that I cared. I needed this dealt with now, and I knew if Emmie Armstrong had Mieke on her payroll, then she was the best of the best at what she did. "Thank you," I told her and hung up just as the text came in.

When I made the call to Mieke, it rang twice before she answered. "Who is this?" she snapped in greeting. "And how the fuck did you get my number?"

"Jordan Moreitti," I introduced myself. "And Mia Barrick gave me the number."

"Mia did?" She grumbled something under her breath I didn't catch, and I didn't care enough to ask her to repeat. "Jordan... Yeah, okay. I remember you. Gabriella's cousin or nephew or whatever. I guess that makes you part of my family, on the rocker side. What can I do for you?"

"How much to have you look for and take down anything...damaging to Arella Stevenson?"

She sighed. "I usually get these requests from Emmie."

"I don't want Emmie or anyone else to know about this," I told her, trying and failing to keep my voice calm. It was hard, though, when I was pissed the fuck off. All I could think about were the sounds Arella made as she'd sucked my cock the day before and how billions of pervs could be listening to that same sound right that moment. "Especially not Drake or Lana Stevenson. Name your price. I'll pay it."

"Dude, just tell me what I'm looking for, and I'll take care of it. Geesh, relax a little before you blow a vessel or something."

"It's..." I clenched my free hand into a fist. "There may be a sex tape of the two of us. Someone put a camera in her dressing room, and—"

"Say no more," she muttered, anger lacing her own voice now. "Fucking sick pricks. I got you covered." I heard the click-clacking of rapid typing and then her sharp inhale. "Okay, this isn't great, but it's not too bad either. Don't freak out. I can get this down in no time."

For the next hour, she stayed on the phone with me until the video was completely erased from the internet. It was already on more than one site, but she not only took it down, she also put up an alert so that if someone tried to upload it again, she would know immediately.

"I actually have some IP information if you want to turn it over to the cops," Mieke told me as the sound of her typing finally stopped. "I'm not some superspy, I can't trace this guy completely, but this might lead that detective you were telling me about in the right direction."

"Email it to me, along with your bill, and I'll pass the information to Kirtner," I told her.

"No charge, Moreitti. Family doesn't have to be blood. If you think about it, we're like cousins or some shit. My mom is Gabriella's manager, and my dad is Liam's band-brother. So yeah, family." I heard her typing again, but this time, it wasn't nearly as rapid. "Email sent. Just forward it to that Kirtner guy, and tell him to contact me if he needs anything else."

"Thank you," I told her again, my muscles starting to relax somewhat for the first time since the detective had called earlier. Now I just had to tell Arella about what had happened.

Fuck.

"You want to thank me, keep Arella safe. This spineless motherfucker obviously wants to hurt her any way he possibly can."

"I swear, I'll protect her with my life."

TWENTY-THREE

ARELLA

TAYLOR WAS BEYOND EFFICIENT IN FINDING JORDAN exactly what he wanted in the person to be my personal assistant. Elliot was fabulous in every aspect. From the way he accessorized to ordering my coffee perfectly and everything in between.

"Girl, those shoes do *not* go with that outfit," he didn't hesitate to inform me as I walked out of the bedroom the first day Taylor brought him to the apartment. "Go change them, or I refuse to be seen with you."

From that moment on, he became my second best friend, and I didn't know what I would do without him. With his eye for detail, his fashion sense, and his mad makeup skills, I thought I might have even fallen a little in love with him. He took care of everything so smoothly that I honestly didn't know how I'd survived without him. While he handled all the work-related details of my life that I didn't have to worry about personally, it left me so much more time in my day-to-day that I actually got more than a hot minute to myself.

And with Jordan almost always around, I was enjoying my personal time even more.

"You have a hair appointment and then a doctor's appointment," Elliot reminded me as we stepped outside the apartment building on one of the rare mornings Jordan had a work meeting. "Both before lunch. And then you promised that adorable sister of yours that you would have lunch with her and the feisty redhead with the delish, beast-like husband."

I lifted my coffee to my lips to keep from laughing at the way Elliot fanned himself every time he spoke about Barrick. Apparently, the overly muscular and hairy type was Elliot's favorite flavor of man-candy. He'd only met Mia and her husband once so far, along with Nevaeh and Braxton, and that had been the week before, but Elliot had been all about Barrick ever since.

It had been three weeks since Elliot had started working for me, and I already wanted to give him a raise. Not only did he take care of my work schedule, but my personal one as well. I'd even arrived on time more often than not, and for that alone, I thought he deserved a bonus at the least.

Thankfully, during that time, there hadn't been any other issues with the stalker. Which was a huge relief after the near miss with the video Mieke was able to keep from going viral. But with that near miss, I'd also given in and let Jordan get me a personal bodyguard.

I didn't like the guy constantly following me around, but he gave Jordan peace of mind when he couldn't be with me, and I had to admit, Samuel did tend to keep the paps back when they tried to get too close. Elliot wasn't too impressed with him, though, and tended to ignore him.

Samuel was the complete opposite of Elliot. Where my personal assistant was slender and beautiful, my bodyguard was barrel-shaped, and his face looked like it was forever frozen in a half snarl that was nothing less than terrifying if you happened to be on the other end of his chilly gaze. He made me feel safe, and that was all that mattered.

"You didn't mention to Jordan or Taylor that I have a doctor's appointment, did you?" I asked as we reached the SUV Jordan had chosen to me. It was built to withstand bullets and chemical warfare—which was ridiculous, but it had made my man grunt his approval when he bought the damn thing. But I knew Jordan was only trying to protect me, so I hadn't put up a fight when he demanded I use the SUV instead of my beloved little car.

Samuel opened the back door for me, and I climbed in. The big man waited until Elliot was in beside me before closing the door and moving around the back of the vehicle to get behind the wheel.

"Girl, you know I don't tell those two shit about fuck if you ask me not to."

"I adore you." Blowing him a kiss, I placed my coffee in the cupholder in front of me.

I'd been having Elliot order me decaf lately, and he'd only grumbled, "You're going to turn into a cranky bitch, but whatevs."

So far, he'd been right. I was cranky without my caffeine, but it looked like I was going to have to go without it for a while.

"How could you possibly not?" he gushed, and like always when he was close by, I couldn't fight my smile.

My hair appointment took all of twenty minutes since all I needed was a simple trim. The stop for the doctor's was longer—and definitely more invasive. I'd missed my period, but I hadn't even realized it until the week before. My doctor hadn't had an opening until this week, and I'd been waiting for this appointment before I told Jordan.

I'd made the appointment myself, then told Elliot it was a regular checkup when I had him add it to my calendar. I might adore him, but there was no way I was going to tell anyone but Jordan first.

While I was in the doctor's office, Elliot and Samuel stayed in the vehicle. Over an hour later, I walked out with my purse full of expectant mommy items that I couldn't wait to show Jordan later. But the appointment had taken longer than expected, and I was late for my lunch date with Nevaeh and Mia.

Elliot and Samuel both joined me as I entered the restaurant. I wasn't the only one of the three of us with a bodyguard. Both Mia and my sister had one that drove them around whenever their husbands weren't available to go with them. It annoyed Nevaeh, but Mia was used to it since she'd had one shadowing her from the time she was five.

"Figured you would be late," Mia said as she stood and embraced me. Her adorable baby bump was hard to miss, and I found myself rubbing my hand over it before she could pull away, while mentally squealing that this was going to be me in only a few short months. "So we ordered drinks and apps."

"Thank goodness. I'm starving." I hugged my sister and then sat beside her while Elliot greeted them both and took the chair beside Mia.

"I knew if Jordan ever got his shit together and you two got together, you would end up with a guard," Nevaeh said with a smirk. "You can't have a billionaire boyfriend and not need some extra muscle."

I gave her a tight smile. "Yup. Jordan brings all the crazies out."

I hated lying to her and everyone else, but I couldn't tell

her that the reason I needed the bodyguard was because I had a stalker. I trusted my sister with a lot of things, but I knew she wouldn't keep this a secret from our parents, and I didn't want to put that kind of stress on them.

Mia was quick to change the subject, telling us about the gender-reveal party her mom was throwing that upcoming weekend. When Jordan told me about the video the stalker had tried to show the world, he'd confessed he'd asked Mia for advice on how to get me to agree to a bodyguard. I hadn't liked that he'd gone behind my back and told her what was going on, but I understood.

Mostly.

At least now I didn't have to feel all territorial and jealous every time I thought about Jordan and Mia. For years, I'd been so jealous of their relationship, but now, I could see it was the same as Mia's relationship with Jagger, and I didn't know how I'd always missed those brother-sister vibes from them.

"Is Emerson excited to be a big sister?" I asked, stuffing a piece of bread into my mouth.

"It's all she talks about," Mia said with a laugh. "But I don't think she understands that this baby isn't like her dolls. She can't just toss it aside when she gets tired of playing with it."

"Do you think she's going to be jealous when she sees you with the new baby?" Nevaeh asked with concern.

Mia snorted. "Me? No. I doubt she would even be jealous over Barrick and the baby either. No, I'm more concerned about how she's going to react to seeing Dad with the baby."

"I'm sure Uncle Nik will handle it," I tried to reassure her.

"Enough about me and the party." Mia put her hand on

Elliot's shoulder. "Tell us, Elliot. Has this one finally decided on a house yet or not?"

He groaned. "Bitch, please. This girl is picky as hell. She loves everything, but she's not *in love* with anything she's been shown. She and that scrumptious man of hers have been looking for three-plus weeks now, and she finds something wrong with everything."

I rolled my eyes at him but grinned. "Hey, I can't help that I have standards."

"You do know there are things called contractors who can remodel houses, right? You didn't like that bathroom in the pool house last week. The bathroom." He pointed his fork at me. "Do you understand that you could have had that small issue resolved in two weeks flat with the kind of cash your man has?"

My sister's eyes grew concerned. "What's wrong, Arie? Why can't you commit to a house?"

"None of them have been our forever home," I told her with a shrug. "I want the perfect place to spend the rest of my life with Jordan. And none of them have been close to that."

"Maybe you should just build your own house," Nevaeh recommended. "Then you can control every detail. All you really have to do is decide where you want to build it."

Jordan had already suggested that, and I'd told him to start looking for an architect, but we'd still been viewing anything Peter had that we might like. I knew Jordan had wanted us to have our house before we found out we were pregnant, but now I would be happy as long as we had it before the baby was born.

The rest of the meal was nothing but girl talk. As the waiter placed my dessert in front of me, Nevaeh's phone rang and she sighed. "It's either Braxton asking when I'll be home or Mom to ask if Conrad can spend the night."

"What's the problem?" I asked with a lifted brow. "You know you don't have to worry when he's with Mom and Daddy, and you and Brax can start working on making the little guy a baby brother or sister."

"Start?" she said with a snort, then slapped her hand over her mouth.

Mia and I both squealed at the same time. "Nevaeh Joy Collins!" I whispered. "Are you pregnant again?"

"Maybe..." She pointed her finger at each of us. "You three better keep that to yourselves. I still don't know for sure, and I haven't told my husband. I'm picking up a test on the way home and taking it. Hopefully before Braxton gets home."

Elliot drew an "X" over his heart. "I'll take it to the grave, girl."

She narrowed her eyes on Mia and then me. "Promise me."

"My lips are sealed," Mia told her, and I nodded.

"This conversation never took place. Now, get your slutty ass home and piss on a stick so we can find out if I'm going to be an auntie again."

She pinched my arm, hard, making me yelp. I slapped her on the ass when she got to her feet. But before she picked up her purse, she bent and put her lips to my ear, hissing, "You're one to talk, hoebag. I saw how your face turned green even as you were stuffing your mouth with those fried pickles."

"Nevi!" I squeaked, turning pleading eyes on her. "Don't you dare!"

"Lips sealed, little sister." She kissed my cheek then

practically skipped out of the restaurant, her bodyguard right behind her.

"What was that about?" Mia asked, watching her go curiously.

"No clue," I lied, and her green eyes narrowed on me. For a second, it almost felt as if it were Aunt Emmie giving me that look, and I picked up my phone so I could avoid her gaze.

I'd put my phone on silent when we'd sat down to eat. The three missed calls and texts from Jordan waiting on me made me smile. I couldn't wait to get home and tell him our news.

TWENTY-FOUR
JORDAN

I knew Arella had a busy morning, so I didn't rush after my meeting. There was something I'd been putting off, but I knew I couldn't do it any longer and still expect Drake Stevenson to respect me.

He and Lana knew I was with their daughter, but as Arella had suspected, he wasn't openly welcoming me into the family like he used to do. I needed to fix that because I knew how important her family was to my girl.

Pulling into the Stevensons' driveway in Santa Monica, I stepped out of my car. The garage door was open, and Drake was standing over a '67 Corvette. It needed to be restored, and Arella told me it was a project her dad had talked about taking on in the past. Lana had bought the old classic for him as a Christmas present, and he'd slowly been working on it since then.

Beside the car sat a pack 'n play where Nevaeh's son was sitting up, chewing on a soft version of his grandfather's expensive new toy. Drake had turned to look at me when I'd first pulled into the driveway, but he'd just as quickly dismissed me and gone back to his task.

Stuffing my hands into my pockets, I walked into the garage. Had I ever been this nervous when having to make multimillion-dollar deals? No, but then again, this was probably the most important deal of my life. If this man didn't give me his blessing, would Arella even marry me? Her parents were important to her, and I knew that her father was her ultimate hero.

"What do you know about emission testing?" Drake asked in greeting as he stared down at the engine of his classic toy.

"I think you don't have to worry about that if the vehicle is a '75 or older in this state," I told him. "But I could be wrong."

"Huh," he grunted. "That's good, I guess."

Conrad spotted me and let out a loud shout. I walked over to him and crouched down. He was a drooling machine, and when he grinned, I saw the flash of a tooth that must have recently come in. "Hey there, little man. Are you helping Grandpa?"

"G-Pop," Drake corrected. "Since Nevi won't let me teach him to play the guitar yet, I figured I needed to find something else we could play with while bonding."

Realizing there was no way to just ease into this conversation, and it didn't look like he was going to help me out in that regard, I pushed down my nervousness and pulled the small box out of my pocket. When I held it out, he stiffened, his blue-gray eyes so much like his daughter's becoming hooded. "I know I've made mistakes in the past few years. I understand why you don't think I'm good enough. But I swear to you, I love Arella with everything inside of me. I want to spend the rest of my life making her happy."

He scrubbed a hand over his face, his gaze still on the ring box in my hand. "I never thought you weren't good enough. Stupid as fuck for letting her slip through your fingers, yeah, but never not good enough." He muttered something vicious under his breath as he turned and stomped a few feet away. "You hurt my little girl repeatedly. I gave you the benefit of the doubt countless times, telling her she just needed to give you a little more time. You were scared, I could see it. Hell, kid, I've been there. I let the love of my life walk away because I was too fucked up in the head to be everything she needed. When you meet the one who turns your whole world upside down but you're not ready, you run scared. I get it."

He made a growling noise deep in his throat and turned to face me. "But then you kept tearing her apart. She deserves better than that, boy."

A knot had filled my throat, choking me, but I quickly swallowed it. "I realize that, and you'll never know how sorry I am. Things got mixed up. Wires got crossed, and I didn't think she cared about me in the same way. So, yeah, I ran scared. For years, because I couldn't stand the thought that she might not love me as much as I love her. But then, someone made me realize how blind I've been. I want to make up all of that wasted time to her." I opened the box, showing him the ring. "Please, sir. Give me your blessing to make all of her dreams come true."

He shook his head, and I felt my gut twist. "She's a strong girl. She can make most of her dreams a reality all by herself. We raised her to stand on her own, to fight for what she wants. That's why she's gotten so far in her career without my help." He inhaled deeply, as if he were in pain, and slowly blew it out. "But you're part of her dream too. And I won't ever stand in the way of any of my babies' happiness." He walked back over to me and thrust out his hand. "You have my blessing, Jordan."

My fingers trembled as I shook his hand, my eyes stinging with tears of gratitude. "Thank you, sir."

His hand tightened around mine. Fuck, it hurt like hell, but I didn't even flinch. I'd take this punishment and anything else he threw at me, as long as I got to keep Arella. Losing her was the only thing that could ever break me. "But if you ever make that girl cry again, I will chop you into tiny pieces and scatter your body from here to Vegas so that your mother won't ever find all of you."

His threat made me want to grin, because it was definitely one I would be using one day if some motherfucker ever dared to make my own daughter cry. "I promise you, Drake. You'll never have to worry about that where Arella is concerned. She loves me, and I'm not strong enough to ever let her go."

A throat clearing behind me had Drake stiffening and dropping his hold on my hand like it was on fire. "Angel, I was just telling the boy—"

Lana snickered as I turned to face her. "I heard most of what you were telling *the boy*, Dray," she chided, walking over to the pack 'n play to lift Conrad out. Straightening, she gave me a wink and turned back to go into the house. "And I'm sure he needs some ice for his hand."

"I'm good," I told her, not even daring to shake out the throb that still lingered in my fingers.

"Dray, baby, get our future son-in-law something to drink while I change this little one. I just called his mom to ask if he could spend the night. Looks like my guys are getting a sleepover tonight." Lana cooed down at Conrad. "Does my little man want to spend the night cuddling with G-Mom?"

"I want to cuddle with G-Mom," Drake called after her, a pout on his face. "Can I cuddle with her too?"

"Only if you get Jordan something to drink and are nice for the rest of the day," she yelled back from the kitchen.

"I can do that, I guess," he grumbled. "You want tea or soda, kid?"

"I should probably head home," I told him as I pocketed the ring box once again. "Need to ask your daughter a pretty important question."

"That can wait another five minutes," he growled at me. "Angel said I have to get you a drink or I can't cuddle with her tonight. You're getting the fucking drink."

Grinning, I followed him into the house. "Is this how it's going to be with Arella? Am I going to have to do exactly as she requests to get cuddles from her too?"

He released an unhappy grunt as he crossed to the fridge and pulled out a bottle of diet soda. "You've met her, right?"

Lana's soft giggle at her husband's question reminded me of Arella's. I hadn't seen her all morning, and I was itching to get back to her. I needed to hear her voice, smell her skin, touch her. I didn't like being away from her for long, but this was important. Now, I ached to be beside her again.

To make my new future in-laws happy, I stayed long enough to finish a drink with Drake before heading back to the apartment where Arella had already texted me she was. The ache in my chest that was always there when we weren't beside each other was pressing down on me, but I tried—and failed—not to speed to get back to her.

By the time I walked into our living room, I was almost gasping for each breath in my need to hold her. "Love?" I called when I didn't see her. "Arella."

"In here!"

I followed the sound of her voice into our bedroom and

found her sitting in the middle of the bed. She had on one of my T-shirts that practically swallowed her, one side hanging low over her shoulder, exposing the top of her breast enticingly, with her hair pulled up into a messy but sexy knot on top of her head. As I walked in, she pushed up onto her knees and held out her arms, welcoming me with a secretive little smile that made my heart clench.

Kicking off my shoes, I grabbed hold of her hips and jerked her against me. "Missed you so damn much," I groaned, burying my face in her neck.

"Babe," she murmured with concern. "You're shaking."

"Can't do this shit anymore, love. I can't spend so many hours without you beside me." My hands slid down to her ass, my fingers digging into the tight muscles of each hip through the shirt. "Nearly lost my mind on the way home because I couldn't breathe without you."

She combed her fingers soothingly through the hair on the back of my head. "It was only one morning, Jord. We're rarely apart."

I clenched my eyes closed. "I know, but I can't think straight when you're away from me. I know I can't be with you every second, twenty-four seven, that I'll smother you if I'm not careful, but there is this weight on my chest when we aren't together that physically hurts."

I felt her lips touch the side of my face. "You couldn't ever smother me, I promise. I want to be close to you every minute of the day. Beside you is my favorite place in the world." One of her hands left my hair and rubbed down my back before reaching behind her and taking hold of one of mine. She guided our hands around her body and placed them over her lower abdomen. "Jordan..."

Something in her voice had my eyes snapping open, and I lifted my head. That secretive little smile was back in place on her lips, and her eyes glittered with tears. "I've been waiting to tell you this for over a week, but I wanted to confirm it with the doctor in case I was wrong." Her tongue brushed over her bottom lip, but for once, she couldn't so easily distract me. Every cell in my body suddenly felt like it was zinging with electricity. "We're pregnant."

I'd thought the day Arella told me she loved me for the first time was the happiest day of my life, but every day since had been even happier than the last. Yet, this moment would be something I remembered when I was ninety and couldn't even remember how to feed myself. I'd never forget the happy tears that made her blue-gray eyes sparkle or the pink flush to her cheeks. The way her smile was so sweet and precious that my heart felt like it could fly out of my chest as I looked down at her and realized that no man could possibly love his woman as much as I loved mine.

My heart was in my throat, making it nearly impossible to swallow, but I forced it down. A hundred different questions filled my head, but all I could get out was, "How are you feeling? Are you okay? Do you need anything?"

Her smile became even more brilliant. "I'm fine. I've had a little bit of nausea, but if anything, my appetite has only increased lately. I'm honestly surprised you haven't noticed the five pounds I've put on already."

My hand that was still clenched at her ass flexed. "Just more of you for me to love, babe." My hand that she was holding low against her belly stroked back and forth lovingly. "You saw the doctor today?" She nodded. "Is the baby okay?"

"Our little nugget is perfect," she said and moved back. Reaching under her pillow, she pulled out a few pictures and excitedly handed them over. "The doctor did an ultrasound, and our sweet little baby is already measuring ahead of schedule." She skimmed her finger over a little black blob area on the picture. "This is him or her. I know you can't really see much of anything, but by the next ultrasound, we will be able to make out everything."

All I could do was stare in awe at the glossy piece of paper. That little blob was our precious little nugget. We'd made him or her with love, and I would spend the rest of my life making sure they and their mother never questioned how much the two of them meant to me.

Something dripped onto the picture I was holding, and it was only then that I realized I was crying. Sniffling, Arella wiped away my tears. "It's okay, babe. I cried when I first saw our nugget too."

I dropped down on my ass and pulled her onto my lap, holding her back to my chest, I lifted the paper closer so we could both see it. "This is the most beautiful picture I've ever seen," I whispered. "I can't take my eyes off it."

"Should we wait and tell our parents?" she asked after a few minutes of us just silently sitting there looking adoringly down at our baby's first picture. "I know some people wait until after the first trimester, but I don't know if I can. I mean, we don't have to tell the entire world yet, but I think it would be nice to tell the grandparents."

Knowing exactly how my mother was going to react to finding out she was going to be a grandmother, I couldn't stop from grinning. "Whatever you want, love. Just tell me who you want told, and I'll make it happen."

She jumped to her knees and turned to face me. "We should do it in a cute way. When Violet told her parents she was pregnant, she got them presents. Uncle Shane's read, "My grandpa rocks harder than yours" or something like that. But I think we should do something that is inclusive to both your parents and mine. Maybe we could have dinner together, and I can get cupcakes with chocolate nameplates on them. Ours can say Mommy and Daddy, and theirs can say grandmother-to-be..." Her nose scrunched up. "Or is that too cheesy? Why are you smiling at me like that?"

I cupped the back of her head and pulled her in for a gentle kiss. "Because you are, without a doubt, the most amazing, most beautiful woman in the world." I kissed the tip of her nose. "You own my heart, Arella. I never knew happiness like this existed until you became mine."

"Jordan," she breathed, tears filling her eyes. "Don't make me cry."

Reaching into my pocket, I pulled out the little ring box, opened it, and held it out to her. I'd wanted to do this in a more romantic way, but I didn't think I could wait another second to ask her and put that ring on her finger. "When I asked your father to give me his blessing earlier today, I promised him I would never make you cry again. Please don't make me break that promise, love."

She gasped and covered her mouth with her hand. "You...you really asked for his blessing?"

"I told you I would," I reminded her.

"Yeah, but..." Dropping her hand, she shook her head, her eyes going to the oval diamond engagement ring glittering brightly in the light. I'd bought the ring while I was in Italy the last time and kept it in my pocket to remind myself why I was working so hard to get back to Arella. "He actually gave you his blessing?"

"He didn't want to at first," I told her honestly. "But then he said that I was part of your dreams and he couldn't stand in the way of making them come true."

"Oh God," she sobbed. "This is real?"

"Baby, please don't cry." I could feel the pressure

returning to my chest, making it hard to breathe again. "Do you not want to marry me? I-if you want to wait, we can."

"No, no, no," she whimpered, shaking her head and causing her tears to drip onto the bed.

My vision blurred as tears filled my eyes. "No, you don't want to wait? Or no, you don't want to…" I couldn't even speak the words. They felt like razor blades in my throat, and with each inhale, they shredded something vital.

Suddenly, she was back in my lap, her legs straddling my hips as she cupped each side of my face in her soft hands. "Jordan, look at me."

I blinked back the wetness from my eyes so I could see her beautiful face. Her own tears hadn't dried yet, but she was smiling. That had to be a good sign.

Please, fuck, please let it be a good sign.

"I love you so much it hurts," she murmured softly. "Of course I'll marry you. And no, I really don't want to wait. I want to get married straightaway. Like, before I develop a baby bump. I don't want to look fat in my wedding dress."

The relief of having the weight disappear off my chest was so intense that I saw spots for a moment. Finally able to draw a deep enough breath, I crushed my mouth against hers in a kiss that branded us both.

TWENTY-FIVE
ARELLA

I FIGURED TELLING OUR PARENTS ABOUT THE upcoming wedding and our pregnancy news all at the same time was the best. That way, no one's feelings would be hurt if we told one set of parentals before the other.

I had Elliot set up a private room at one of my favorite restaurants and then went in to speak to the chef personally to tell him what I wanted to do to surprise the grandparents. It didn't take more than a few bats of my lashes to talk him into doing a special dessert for my little bitty dinner party. That probably wasn't the only reason, as I suspected my doting fiancé had made a call beforehand to grease the man's palms in order to get me what I wanted, but I was going to pretend it was my own doing.

Afterward, I rushed home so I could get ready for our big surprise dinner. Jordan was taking a meeting with a team of producers from a different studio, and I'd already given Elliot the rest of the day off, so it was only me in the back of the SUV on the way home.

My bodyguard pulled into the garage and drove straight for my usual parking place. I was so excited about dinner that I didn't even think about his rule that I stay in the vehicle until he made sure the surrounding area was safe and he opened the door for me. Humming to myself, I stepped out into the garage and took two steps toward the elevator.

That was as far as I got before a hand clamped over my mouth from behind and I was jerked back against someone. I screamed into the person's palm, realizing from the size of it that it was a man's.

"Release her," I heard Samuel command.

I was suddenly turned so that I was facing Samuel, and I felt something sharp touch my stomach. A sudden sting and then the feel of blood dripping from the wound on my abdomen made me scream into the palm again, and I looked at my bodyguard with overwhelming fear in my eyes, silently pleading with him to help me. Whoever had grabbed me had a very deadly knife from the feel of it, and he was holding it right against my stomach.

Oh God, please don't let anything happen to my little nugget.

Samuel had a gun pointed at the person holding me, his hands steady as he kept it trained several inches above my head. I hadn't even realized he carried a gun. They scared me, but at that moment, I was glad he had it. "Release her," he barked again, his voice never wavering as he took a step closer.

The knife pressed deeper into my flesh, and tears began to spill from my eyes. I didn't even feel the pain, but the fear of something happening to my unborn baby made me shake.

"You have until the count of ten to release her, or I'm going to put a bullet in your brain," Samuel threatened.

A muffled laugh left the person holding me. The sound vibrated through their chest and made my already pounding heart quake with fear. "I don't think so," he said in a voice that was harsh but just as muffled as his laugh.

Samuel took another step toward us, but the knife that was cutting into my belly was suddenly pressed to my throat. I swallowed the next scream that bubbled up, knowing that as sharp as that big knife was, the action of screaming would cause him to slit my throat effortlessly.

"Take another step closer," my assailant dared. "See if I don't slit her open from ear to ear."

Samuel stopped and actually took a step backward, but he was only a blurry form in front of me as my tears began to fall faster.

Was this the stalker who had sent the packages and destroyed my dressing room? Was this the same person who had tried to ruin my career by posting that video of me with Jordan?

Anger filled me, but fear kept me motionless. It wasn't just me that I had to worry about. If something happened to me, that would put my precious baby in danger.

My hand moved to cover the bleeding wound on my abdomen. From the feel of it, I was bleeding pretty badly with how wet and sticky my fingers were. I wanted to stomp on the man's foot and elbow him in the gut the way Luca and Lyric had taught me when we were kids, but the blade pressed so tightly into my skin kept me from so much as swallowing for fear of him slitting my throat.

"All right." Samuel's voice was lower now, as if he were actually trying not to be as intimidating, but the way his lips were snarled back didn't make a difference to how low or soft he made his voice. He was a scary motherfucker to look at. "Let's just stay calm." I thought he was talking more to me than to the man holding a knife against me, because I was the only one shaking in fear. "Tell me what you want.

I'll make it happen. Her fiancé is a rich man. He will pay you any amount you want, give you anything you can think of, as long as you don't harm her."

"Fiancé," the man at my back spat out as if repeating the word left a bitter taste on his tongue. Even through whatever was muffling his mouth, I could hear how much he hated that word. "Moreitti can't have her. She's. Mine." He trailed the blade up and down my throat like a caress, almost...lovingly. "She's my little bird."

"Please," I dared to beg against his hand, but he couldn't understand me, and the action caused the knife to scrape the flesh of my neck raw. It stung, but at least I didn't feel any blood.

He released the hand over my mouth, but only so he could grab my hair. My head was jerked back, and it was a small relief not to have the blade so close to my throat. But it was short-lived as he pulled my head back until his gaze locked with mine.

The man was wearing something similar to a ski mask. All I could see of his face was the area over his eyes and part of his nose. Even through my tears, I could see his eyes as clear as day. Eyes I knew as if I were staring into my own.

Pop-Pop's eyes.

Mom's eyes.

Garon Steel's eyes.

"Why?" I whispered, not understanding.

How could he have sent those packages? Those disgusting pictures of him jerking himself off with my favorite lotion... I felt even sicker now than I had when I'd first seen those photos. That... That man in those pictures was my uncle?

"You're mine," he gritted out again from behind his mask. "She got everything when the old man died. *Every-*

thing. If I take you, one of her precious children, and make you mine, it will destroy her." The knife touched my cheek, again in a tender, adoring kind of way, but the blade scraped over my cheek, and I flinched at the rawness that was left behind.

She? As in...my mom?

"I've watched you, little bird." His voice had turned gentle, but the look in his eyes remained manic. "I've waited and dreamed of the day I would take you. I thought it would have been easier. If you had just taken that part in that fucking movie, things would have gone so much smoother. I could have gone on watching you like I have in the past for a little longer before I had to steal you away."

His hold on my hair tightened, and I could actually feel strands being pulled out of my scalp as his honey-golden eyes darkened with anger. "But no," he seethed, the tenderness evaporating from his voice. "No, you wouldn't take the part! And then there was Moreitti. I thought I could use him, get him to make you see it was good for your career, but that little pencil-dick loser couldn't even do that." Garon lowered his head until his lips were almost touching mine, and I felt bile lift into my throat. "Did you think of me while you fucked him, little bird? Did you imagine it was my cock you were riding?"

This wasn't happening, I thought as I cowered back from him. This sick man couldn't be saying these vile things to me. It was wrong, so very wrong. I whimpered in fear, wanting this moment erased from my mind.

Everything happened so fast, I didn't even have time to blink. A sudden shot filled the garage. One moment, Garon was about to kiss me, and then the next, part of his head was missing.

The knife fell to the ground, but I didn't hear it or

anything else. The blast of the gunshot hurt my ears, the sound making them ring so badly that I couldn't even hear the blood rushing through my veins like I had only moments before.

Blood was splattered on my face and clothes. There was something thick dripping from my hair. All of that barely registered as Garon dropped lifelessly at my feet.

I bent in half, retching.

Strong arms came around me, and I tried to look up to see who it was.

Braxton?

My brother-in-law tucked my head against his chest as he carried me away from my uncle's dead body.

TWENTY-SIX
ARELLA

I DIDN'T UNDERSTAND WHAT WAS GOING ON AROUND me, could barely hear the voices as people talked rapidly to one another, into their phones, or to me. I was sitting in the open doors of an ambulance as a nice female paramedic cleaned the blood and brain matter off my face. She'd already bandaged the wound on my belly and told me I was going to have to go to the hospital for stitches, but it wasn't a life-and-death injury, so we had a little time.

At least that was what I'd heard through the continued ringing in my ears, so I wasn't completely sure that was exactly what she'd said. But we weren't rushing to the hospital.

Braxton stood close by, limping as he paced back and forth, talking into his cell phone. To whom, I had no idea, but the look on his face told me he wasn't happy. Samuel stood beside the ambulance, his eyes constantly moving around the garage as if everyone was a threat.

The cops were standing by Garon's dead body. A sheet had been thrown over him, and several people had lifted it a few times to inspect the damages.

Braxton had killed Garon.

How he'd even known I needed help, I had no idea, but I was thankful.

"Arella!"

The roar of my name broke through the ringing in my ears, and I lifted my head to find Jordan running toward me.

His face was as pale as a ghost, his suit jacket missing, his tie hanging loose around his neck, and the sleeves of his shirt rolled up to his elbows. He looked ragged and scared, and I'd never seen a more wonderful sight in my life.

With a cry, I jumped from the back of the ambulance and threw myself into his arms. Sobbing, I buried my face in his chest and held on to him for dear life.

Jordan trembled as he ran his hands over me. "Thank God you're okay," he said as he tilted my head up so he could kiss me. "When your mom called me, I nearly had a heart attack."

"My mom?" I repeated. "Not Samuel?"

"He did," he confirmed, his quivering hands running up and down my body. "But Lana's call came first."

"I don't understand. Why would she call you? How would she even know?"

"Arie!"

"Arella!"

At the unmistakable sound of my parents calling my name, I turned my head to find them both being led into the garage by one of Braxton's men, Barrick right behind them. Both of them looked just as stressed as Jordan, and that was the last thing I'd wanted.

"Oh no," I whimpered, and I felt the world begin to spin. "Brax must have told them."

"Arella." Jordan's arms tightened around me just as my legs gave out. "Baby!" he roared. Lifting me into his arms, he carried me back to the ambulance that was thankfully a good distance away from my rapidly approaching parents. "Are you sure she's okay? She's pregnant."

"She mentioned that," the sweet paramedic said with a reassuring smile. "Other than needing a few stitches, she's fine. But I think the adrenaline might finally be leaving her, so she's quite possibly going to crash at any moment."

My head rolled against Jordan's chest, and then I felt my mother's soft fingers touching my cheek. "Arella," she murmured. "Honey, it's okay. You're safe now."

I blinked my eyes and almost flinched when I met her gaze before remembering these honey-gold eyes belonged to the woman I loved most in the world. "Mommy," I sobbed. "He...he was crazy."

"I know, sweetheart. I'm so sorry. We had no clue it was Garon." She pushed my hair back from my face but quickly pulled back her hand and stared down at her palm in a mixture of fascination and horror. "Is that...? Oh God."

She began to sway, but my dad was there to steady her. Lifting her into his arms, he barked at the paramedic to get out of his way. The woman quickly did as he commanded, and he carried my mom into the back of the ambulance to lay her on the gurney. "Take it easy, Angel. It's okay," he soothed, stroking her hair back from her face. "Braxton took care of it. Garon isn't a threat to her any longer. She's safe, Angel. She's safe."

I wasn't sure if he was trying to ease Mom's fear or his own, but listening to them broke my heart. Putting them through something like this was what I'd wanted to avoid, yet there they were, trying to stay calm even though the danger was now gone.

"Dray, his brains are in her hair!" Mom cried. "We have to get her cleaned up. Let me up. I'll take her to their apartment and help her shower. She can't go around with his brains in her hair."

Jordan carried me into the already cramped interior of the ambulance and sat me on the end of the gurney with Mom. Crouching down in front of me, he silently took the towel Samuel offered him and began to finish cleaning the gore out of my hair that the paramedic had missed.

It took every ounce of strength I still had just to sit upright, but I did it because I didn't want to freak out my parents any more than they already were. "I-I'm sorry," I whispered in an unsteady voice. "I didn't want you two to have to worry about me. There hadn't been any issues since the dressing room incident, so I thought maybe he'd stopped."

"What dressing room incident?" my dad demanded.

Jordan's eyes met mine, and I gave a nod at the unasked question in his. "Someone destroyed her dressing room on the last day of filming. I'm assuming it was Garon. The detective found part of a device that suggested there had been a camera hidden in there, and I guess he'd been spying on her for a while."

I was thankful he didn't mention what Garon had done with the footage from that camera.

"There've also been packages delivered," I told them after a small hesitation, wanting to tell them everything so they had the full story. "Murdered little birds, messages..." My stomach turned. "Pictures of him doing...things to himself."

"He sent you shit too?" Mom yelled.

I blinked a few times before her question finally registered. "I'm sorry, what do you mean 'too'?"

She pressed her lips together and quickly looked away, but not before I saw the guilt on her beautiful face.

"Mom?" I breathed, but she wouldn't look at me, so I focused on my dad. "Daddy?"

Running his hands through his long hair, he crouched down beside Jordan and took one of my hands. "I know we should have told you, and I'm so sorry now that we didn't. But you had so much going on the last few months. The show was ending, and you seemed so caught up in trying to decide which part to take next. Between that and still seeming so sad after Cole's death and Jordan being a dumbass, we just didn't want to add more to your stress level, Arie."

I shook my head in denial. "Are you saying you knew I had a stalker?"

"Your mom was getting letters and packages. Things taped to the window of her car or random boxes left at our front door. We gave it all to Braxton and swore him to secrecy and then asked him to put a secret security team on you. Not even Nevaeh or Barrick knew. Only lately, the letters had gotten more threatening, and we were so relieved when Jordan hired Samuel for you. But we thought it was only because he's so possessive. We had no idea that you were having issues with the stalker too."

"You should have told me!" I cried.

His blue-gray eyes narrowed. "Oh yeah? Like you told us about what was going on with you?"

Guilt and shame hit me, and I lowered my eyes to the towel in Jordan's hand. The starkness of the blood and brain matter against the white cloth turned my stomach, so I quickly looked away.

Straight back into my dad's eyes.

"I'm sorry," I whispered.

"Us too, sweetheart." He tucked a few locks of my hair behind my ear and thankfully didn't encounter anything slimy in the process. "The last letter showed up a few days ago, and Braxton started shadowing you himself. He saw Garon outside your building and followed him into the garage. That's when he called us. We didn't realize it was Garon until today. But after he stopped contesting Cole's will so abruptly, we should have suspected he had something else up his sleeve."

I shuddered, remembering how he'd tried to kiss me, the things he'd said.

I only wanted to forget this entire day.

"Okay, folks, we should get going now that the cops have given the go-ahead for her to leave the scene," the paramedic said as she appeared at the back of the ambulance beside Samuel. "Um, technically, I can only let one of you ride with us, and we tend to let daddies ride with mommies-to-be."

I let out a disappointed whine at her spilling my secret just as my parents started yelling at the same time.

"What the fuck do you mean daddies? The only daddy in here is me!" my dad bellowed at the woman. "And you're damn right I'm going to be riding with my baby girl."

"You're pregnant!" Mom exclaimed, throwing her arms around me. "Oh, sweetheart, is that why we were having dinner with the Moreittis tonight? Oh my goodness! Are you okay?" She started running her hands over me frantically now. "Are you sure he didn't hurt you?"

"I just need stitches, Mom," I assured her.

"Where?" Her eyes scanned over every part of me she could see but wasn't able to find a wound bad enough to need medical attention.

Biting my lip, I pulled up my shirt to show them the deep gash on my lower abdomen. It was the first time Jordan had seen it too, and my gaze went straight to his face.

I could see the banked rage in his eyes and the set of his jaw, but he kept his mouth shut and just held my hand a little tighter.

"That motherfucker better be glad he's dead," Daddy snarled.

"Dray." Mom put her hand on his arm, trying to soothe him, but there was no mistaking the tremble in her voice when she spoke again. "It's okay. She...she just needs a few stitches. We'll meet them at the hospital."

It took a few more minutes, but she eventually got him out of the ambulance. I heard Jordan tell Samuel to follow us in the SUV before the ambulance driver closed the door on us. Through the window, I saw my parents walking out of the garage with Barrick and Braxton, who was still on the phone.

Jordan, kissing my hand that was held tightly in his, pulled my gaze back to him. With my free hand, I combed my fingers through his hair. "I'm okay," I told him again, but the world was going dark around the edges.

I tried to blink my eyes to clear my vision, but when they closed, they wouldn't open again.

TWENTY-SEVEN
JORDAN

Getting the frantic call from Lana that Arella was in danger was something that would haunt me for the rest of my life. I didn't think I could ever hear a phone ring again without feeling a shot of the fear I'd felt when I thought I might have lost my reason for living.

I'd thought one bodyguard would be enough. It was our compromise when I asked her to take personal security seriously. She'd given in, but only allowed me to get her one guard. I should have just gotten her twenty and dealt with the consequences of her being pissed at me.

Maybe then, I wouldn't have had to wipe brains out of her hair, or nearly lost my mind all over again when she showed me the deep cut low on her belly where the sonofabitch had hurt her with a knife. The realization that I'd come so close to losing not only Arella but our little nugget made it hard to breathe. Trying to hold on to my control, I pushed it all down while we were at the hospital and on the drive home.

I'd texted my parents at Arella's request to reschedule our family dinner with the Stevensons. I hadn't told them what was going on, and that was probably a good thing. My mom freaking out while Arella's parents were already on edge would have been too much for my girl right then.

Samuel pulled into the garage but didn't immediately get out. I kissed Arella's forehead, but she was still sound asleep. After she'd passed out in the ambulance on the ride to the hospital, she'd woken up a few times, but it had been difficult for her to keep her eyes open. The doctor had warned me that she might be exhausted for a few days, given the trauma she'd been through.

"I'll understand if you want to fire me, Mr. Moreitti," Samuel said after a full minute had passed.

"Braxton told me everything that happened."

I'd had to suffer through those details, but there was no way I could handle not knowing the specifics. I knew that Samuel had done everything he was supposed to. That he'd pointed a gun at Garon Steel's head until the blade of the knife he'd used on her had been placed against her throat. He'd tried to distract Garon, talk to him, but all the deranged man had been focused on was Arella.

Thankfully, Braxton had gotten an opening and been able to take him out.

"You did a good job today. I'm thankful you kept a clear head and did what you could to protect her." My arms tightened around her. "But expect a partner tomorrow. Maybe two. It's not that you aren't good at your job. I just don't think I can let her go anywhere without me unless she has an army surrounding her now."

Samuel gave a stiff nod. "Yes, sir. I understand."

He got out and opened my door. I had to force myself to release Arella long enough to step out, and then I was lifting her into my arms and carrying her up to our apartment.

The need to find us a house was even more urgent now.

I had to get her out of this place so the memories of what had happened in that garage earlier didn't haunt either one of us.

"Jordan?" she mumbled sleepily as we entered the apartment.

"Right here, baby," I told her, kissing her forehead again. "We're home."

Her eyes popped open. "Thank goodness. I want a shower so bad. I can't go to bed with..." She broke off with a shudder.

"Don't worry, love. I'll help you." I carried her straight into the bathroom. Setting her on the sink, I carefully pulled off her shirt and then got rid of her pants, leaving her in only her bra and panties as I went to turn on the shower.

The doctor had told us not to submerge her incision in water, but she could shower as long as she kept her back to the spray. While the water heated, I walked back to her. She opened her legs invitingly, and I stepped between them. But instead of kissing her as I could see she wanted, I only cupped my hand over her belly, reassuring myself that she and our baby were still there.

Both of them were safe.

"I'm really okay," she murmured again, when the silence became too much for her. "You don't have to worry about us now."

I pressed my forehead to hers. "If I'd lost you today, I wouldn't be alive right now."

"Don't say that," she cried.

"It's the truth." I cupped her face in both of my hands. "I don't want to live in a world where you don't exist. If I'd lost you—"

"But you didn't." She took one of my hands and pressed

it to her heart, letting me feel how fast it was beating. "I'm right here, and I'm not going anywhere."

"I know, baby. Just..." I closed my eyes and inhaled deeply before slowly releasing it. "Just give me a little time to get a hold on what I'm feeling right now. I might be a little overbearing for a while. Don't hold that against me."

She pushed on my chest until I pulled back enough for us to lock eyes. "I'm okay with you being overbearing. I'm even okay with you keeping me locked up in this apartment for a few days. But what I'll never be okay with is you not kissing me."

I stroked my thumb over her bottom lip. "Once I kiss you, I won't be able to stop, and you need to rest."

"No," she growled, and the sound was so sexy, my cock nearly broke through the seam of my slacks. "What I need is for my man to fuck me until neither one of us can keep our eyes open."

"Baby, let me get you clean first." I lifted her and carried her into the shower.

Washing her from head to toe without pushing her up against the wall of the stall and fucking her until she couldn't remember anything but me took a willpower I didn't even know I possessed. It was even harder when she pouted up at me, whining for a kiss.

Once we were both clean, I turned off the water and wrapped a towel around my waist before grabbing another to dry her with. When she was no longer dripping, I carried her to our bed and placed her carefully in the center. "Are you hungry?" It was getting late, and we hadn't eaten anything all evening.

"Yes," she snapped and grabbed hold of my towel. It disappeared over her shoulder, and then she was pulling me down onto the bed beside her.

"I need to feed you," I tried to argue. I needed her so fucking badly, but if I touched her at that moment, kissed her as she was begging for, I knew I would lose control.

"I need *you*," she bit out and pushed me onto my back with surprising strength. Tossing her damp hair over her shoulder, she straddled me. Her drenched pussy brushed over my straining cock as she bent her head and touched her lips to mine ever so softly. "I need to feel you inside me. I need you to erase all the bad memories of this day and replace them with every part of you surrounding me. I need you to remind us both that I'm here and safe."

"I could hurt you." I was losing what hold I had on my control with each passing second. "What if I pop one of your stitches?"

"You're hurting me right now," she whispered with a quaver in her voice. "I ache for you, and you're denying me what I need the most in the world. Why, Jordan? Why? Don't you want me?" She pressed herself against my cock harder. "I can feel how much your body wants me, but do your heart and head not want me anymore?"

"No, baby, no." Carefully, I cupped her ass and rolled us so I was between her spread thighs. She wrapped her legs around me, trapping me, as if she thought I would leave her if she didn't. Brushing the hair back from her face, I saw the glitter of tears in her eyes and groaned. The sight of her crying was pure agony to me. "I want every inch of you—body, heart, and soul. I'm just scared…"

"Of what?" she asked as a tear spilled over her lashes. "I promise, if anything hurts, I'll let you know."

"I don't want to scare you," I confessed. "Braxton told me that Garon tried to kiss you. That you were scared of him."

"I was scared of him," she admitted with a tiny nod,

another tear spilling over and sliding down her pale cheek. "But I don't have to worry about him trying to hurt me again. He's gone now, unable to hurt me or anyone else ever again. And even if he weren't dead, it wouldn't matter. Because there is nothing you could ever do that would scare me, Jordan." She arched her hips, rubbing herself against my shaft. "You could hold me down and fuck me as hard as you wanted right this minute, and I would only beg you for more."

"Baby," I groaned, feeling the last thread of my control starting to snap.

"I need you inside me, Jordan," she whimpered. "I need you to show me how much you love me. How much it hurts not to be beside me every second of the day. I need you to own my body."

"Fuck," I roared, and I thrust into her hot, wild heat.

"Yes," she screamed, her head tossed back in ecstasy. "That's it, babe. I belong to you. Every inch of me is yours. Own me. Please, own me."

I tried to be gentle, but I no longer had control over my own body. Once I felt her sweet pussy squeezing around my shaft, I was lost.

She begged me to own her, but we both knew she was the one who owned me.

TWENTY-EIGHT
JORDAN

It was almost a week later before I could even bring myself to let Arella out of bed, let alone out of the apartment. During that time, I told Barrick to get me two more guards for Arella. I didn't plan on not being with her when she did leave the apartment, but I knew she would eventually have to go somewhere without me, and I needed a small army protecting her when that happened.

After our first week of self-imposed lockdown, we didn't have much alone time. Between her parents and mine, her siblings, and then Mia, Elliot, Taylor, and Palmer popping in almost every day, we were rarely left alone.

Once Garon Steel's death hit the news, my parents had found out what happened. And when they couldn't reach me, they called Lana and Drake. During that first call, Lana must have let slip that Arella was pregnant, and the two of them had been at our place every day since I'd first let either of them through the door.

My girl was disappointed that she hadn't gotten to surprise them with our baby announcement, but part of me was glad I didn't have to keep it from my mom and dad until she was ready to have our dinner with all the parents.

"You know," Arella murmured as she tucked her feet up under her on the couch. "Garon can't do that villainess movie now. I mean, maybe he can do his own version in hell where he's rotting right now, but not here in the real world."

I wrapped my arm around her, glad she could speak about her uncle without it bothering her. I'd worried that seeing him die right in front of her would leave some lingering psychological damage, but so far, she'd been recovering from the trauma of it all like a champ. "Yeah?"

"Yeah," she murmured and climbed onto my lap. Thankfully, we had the place all to ourselves this evening. "Winston Cline emailed me earlier, saying something about taking on all of Garon's open projects. I'm going to assume that the movie Garon wanted you to back him on will be one of them." She stroked her index finger down my nose. "And if you can talk Winston into waiting until after the baby is born and I've lost the weight I'm already putting on, I'd be okay with taking on the lead role in the franchise."

I dropped my hand to her belly. "If that's what you want, my love. I'm on board with whatever you say."

She tilted her head back. "Is that one house Peter was talking about still on the market?"

"Be more specific, baby. Poor Peter has talked about a lot of houses with us," I reminded her with a smirk.

Arella bit her lip for a moment before releasing it. "The house near Mia. The mansion with twenty-thousand square feet."

I started tracing little circles on her belly. "You said it was too much house for us."

"I did," she agreed. "But then I started thinking about all the kids we want. And then how much your parents and mine will constantly be at our house visiting. Then I thought about how sometimes I want to suck your dick or have you fuck me at crazy times of the day." She pouted. "And they are always around. If we lived there, and they were in the house, I could take you to the opposite side of the house and still be as loud as I want while you—"

I grabbed my phone before she could even finish that last sentence. Peter picked up on the second ring. "Is that house in Beverly Hills still available?" I demanded while Arella buried her face in my neck and giggled.

"There are three people in a bidding war over it, actually. It's already two million over the asking price," the real estate agent informed me.

"Tell the owners I'll pay them double what they are asking."

Stunned silence filled my ear before he spoke in a strangled voice. "I'll... Um, I will let them know. Expect my call."

I hung up without responding and dropped the phone onto the couch beside us. "It's ours," I told her.

"I heard," she giggled again. The sound warmed something deep inside me that only she could touch. "Good thing my fiancé is a billionaire, or I might have to do a few more movies before this little nugget arrives so we can afford such an expensive home."

"Baby, if you wanted a house the size of the moon on top of Mount Everest, I would make it happen," I vowed.

She cuddled close, her breathing starting to even out, and I thought she was falling asleep until she jumped to her feet. "Oh my goodness! I can't wait to start decorating our home. I have so many ideas for the living room. And our bedroom..."

I sat back, smiling as she paced back and forth in front of me, telling me all about her ideas for our new house. The animation on her face, the way her blue-gray eyes danced with happiness and excitement, only made my heart feel like it was going to fly right out of my chest. Every time she turned to pace in the opposite direction, the light would catch on her engagement ring, and the possessive monster deep inside me purred in contentment.

That ring, and the baby bump that would be showing soon enough, told the world who this woman belonged to.

"Don't tire yourself out too much decorating the house, baby," I warned. "We still have a wedding to plan."

"Our moms are helping with that already," she said with a wave of her hand. "And Aunt Emmie has already found us a venue. I just need to find the perfect dress, and then we're all set."

As she walked in front of me again, I grabbed her by the hips and lifted her onto my lap once again. "How about helping me decide where to go on our honeymoon, then. Where does my beautiful bride want to go?"

"I don't care," she said with a shrug. "Because wherever we end up, I don't plan on us seeing more than the hotel room for the most part."

"Oh yeah?" I murmured, tugging her pajama bottoms down so I could feel the warm flesh of her luscious ass. "And why is that, my bride?"

She smiled coyly. "Because I'm going to spend the entire honeymoon fucking my husband until he's brain-dead from lack of blood supply to his big head."

"How is that different from any other day?" I teased.

She lowered her head until her lips were ghosting over mine. "Because then you will be all mine. Completely at my mercy. With my ring on your finger, tying you to me for the rest of our lives."

I caught the back of her head, taking the kiss she was

trying to deny me. When I let her up for air, I lightly smacked her perfect ass. "Again, other than the ring, how is that different from any other day?" I stroked over the flesh I'd just marked. "I can put a ring on right now if you want. We don't have to have the ceremony for me to wear the ring that will show the world I belong to you just as much as you belong to me."

Her eyes widened. "Really?"

"Yes, really. Whatever ring you want, I'll never take it off."

"What if the ring I want you to wear isn't really a ring?" She started nibbling on her bottom lip again, and with a groan, I used my thumb to tug the tortured flesh free.

"Then you need to tell me what it is so I can make it happen, baby."

"Well..."

"Arella," I bit out. "Tell me, and we'll go get it right now."

"It's just that I don't know how you would feel about... needles." She looked at me through her lashes. "You don't have any ink, and I'd never really asked if that was because you don't want to mark your skin or if you just had an aversion to needles."

"A tattoo?" She nodded. "You want me to get a ring tattoo?"

"Only if you want to. It's just so much more permanent than a regular ring. You can never take it off... Well, I guess you could if you had it lasered off, but—"

I kissed her again to stop her rambling. This woman was so endearingly precious that I would have let her talk me into inking my entire body if that were what she told me she wanted.

Lifting my head, I tucked her hair back behind her ear.

"Your name will look perfect inked around my finger," I told her. "Do you think your cousin Lyric will do it for me if we fly up tonight?"

"He kind of loves me, so I'm sure it won't be a problem," she said with a smile that lit up the room.

"No one could ever love you as much as I do," I growled, that possessive monster roaring to life. "Now, go pack an overnight bag. We'll fly up and be back by tomorrow night."

EPILOGUE

ARELLA

"Deep breath," the nurse instructed. Her touch was gentle on my bare back, soothing and calming my frayed nerves as the anesthesiologist worked on placing the epidural in position.

I was two weeks past my due date, and I still hadn't started dilating on my own, so my doctor had scheduled me for an induction. I'd already had fluids through an IV for over an hour and they were about to give me the meds that would get things started, but before all the fun pain started, they'd asked if I wanted an epidural or not.

Um, yeah, I might have a high pain tolerance, but I wasn't brave enough to go through all that discomfort without drugs, so the epidural had been part of my birthing plan from day one. I didn't really care that my mother had birthed five babies completely naturally, or that my cousin Lyric's wife Mila had nearly ripped herself in half pushing her twin sons out with not a single drop of drugs.

That was great and I applauded them, but I wasn't either of them. This was my experience, and I wanted to enjoy it without screaming and shouting at the people I loved in the throes of agonizing pain.

Plus, I didn't want to have to put Jordan through watching me go through that. It would only make this miserable for us both.

Once the epidural was in place and I was able to lie back on my big comfy hospital bed, surrounded by my own pillows, the nurse let Jordan and our moms back into the room. Apparently after one too many fainting spells from bystanders, the birthing center's policy was no one but the patient and medical staff in the room while an epidural was being administered.

My husband hadn't been happy that he'd had to leave my side, but I was more than a little thankful he wouldn't have to see that.

As soon as he was through the door, Jordan sprinted to my side, kissing me as if he hadn't seen me in weeks instead of less than half an hour. "Are you okay?"

"I'm good," I assured him with a bright smile. Now that the scary part of having a huge needle put in my spine was over, I was great.

While the moms got comfortable in the chairs around my bed, the nurse was already placing the medicine into my IV that would get my labor started. For the next few hours, I sat up in bed and played board games with Mom and Alexis while Jordan rubbed my shoulders and neck. Other members of our family came and went, promising they would be with my dad and Jared Moreitti in the waiting room, where the moms had banished them because neither one of them could handle the anticipation of what was going on in my private laboring room.

Six hours in, the doctor came in and broke my water then said he was going for some dinner.

But no sooner had he reached the door than I started feeling an intense pressure in my lower abdomen and bottom. "Aw, fuck!" I cried, my hands gripping the rails of my bed.

"What?" Jordan cried, his face turning gray. "Baby, what's wrong."

"Well then," the doctor said calmly as he came back to my bed and pressed the nurse's call button. "Let's just take another look, shall we?"

I heard Mom and Alexis murmuring excitedly to each other while Jordan scrubbed his hands over his tired face. "Is she okay?" he demanded just as the two nurses came into the room. They didn't even approach me, just started prepping.

"Arella, take a deep breath for me," my doctor said in that soothing voice he was known for. "Jordan, why don't you help her pull her knees up to her chest."

I felt my husband's hands tremble as he did as he was instructed. Mom came around to my other side and helped too while Alexis moved to stand beside her son. Another intense pain hit me and I tried not to cry out, but it was too much and I whimpered just as the doctor told me to push.

Two more and then the room was filled with the angelic cry of my beautiful baby girl. She was placed on my chest, and the grandmothers started sobbing. "She's so beautiful," Alexis cried, her hand rubbing over the baby's thick, dark hair. "Hello, little beauty. I'm your nonna."

The baby started snuffling around my chest, and I helped her find her way to my breast, in complete and total awe at how beautiful she truly was. I couldn't take my eyes off her even to blink. All that dark hair Mom had warned me she would have because my heartburn had been ridiculously horrible. I saw myself in the shape of her nose, lips, and even her jaw. Her fingers and toes were so tiny, I felt like I was holding one of my baby dolls from when I was a little girl.

Jordan left my side long enough to cut the umbilical cord, and then the nurses were taking the baby to the other side of the room to check her over while the doctor took care of me.

"Can you feel that?" Jordan asked in a strangled voice.

I frowned up at him. "Feel what?"

"He's got his arm inside you up to his elbow," he rasped out, looking even more gray in the face than he had earlier.

"Just helping the placenta out," my doctor said as he finally rolled his chair back and placed something in a medical pan. "You did great, Arella. Not a single tear."

Mom brushed my hair back from my face. "Didn't even break a sweat," she said with pride in her voice. "I'm going to go tell your dad that you're okay and he's finally got his granddaughter."

I grinned. After Nevaeh and Braxton announced they were having another boy, Daddy had started grumbling that all he was going to have were grandsons. Not that he truly minded. He adored Conrad and Carver, who was only three weeks old now. But he'd been hinting that he hoped I was having a girl. Jordan and I had known for months we were expecting a daughter, but we'd wanted to surprise everyone with the baby's sex since we hadn't gotten to do the surprise-we're-expecting dinner the day Garon had tried to take me.

Alexis took one last longing look at her granddaughter before saying she was going to go tell Jared, giving me a wink as she followed Mom out the door. I knew she was giving us a moment alone, or as alone as we could be with the nurses and doctor still tending to our baby girl and me.

Jordan brushed a kiss over my forehead. "You did so great, Mommy."

"I couldn't have done it without your help, Daddy."

He snorted. "I didn't do much of anything."

"No, babe, you were a great leg holder," I teased and tugged him down for a quick kiss. My heart felt full to the point of bursting, and it was all thanks to him. "We finally get to tell everyone her name," I murmured sleepily. "I can't believe I was able to keep it a secret this whole time so that no one would know we were having a girl."

"I was just about to ask if we had a name," one of the nurses spoke up as they finished swaddling our precious baby. "What should I put on her chart?"

"Braelyn Angelica Moreitti," Jordan told her, then spelled it out for the woman so she could get it right for the baby's birth certificate.

It was a few hours later before we could have visitors. Jordan's mom sat in the rocking chair near the window, and Mom placed Braelyn in her arms. The pure joy on Alexis's face was too much to witness, and I had to blink back my happy tears.

"Hello, sweet Braelyn," she murmured softly. The baby looked wide awake, her little mouth forming a tiny "o" while she stared up at her paternal grandparents as they gazed down at her in complete awe.

"You were right, *dolcezza*," Jared said in a quiet voice as he touched his finger over the baby's cheek. "She is the most beautiful baby I've ever seen."

"How are you feeling?" my dad asked, his eyes running over my face in concern.

"I feel great," I assured him with a tired smile. "I'm already thinking of how many more times I can do this."

"No," Jordan growled, shaking his head as he looked up

from watching his mom with our daughter. "This is enough."

"But you promised we could fill up our house with all the babies I wanted," I reminded him with a grin.

"I don't like seeing you in pain," he grumbled.

"I felt pain for like two seconds," I waved him off, only half teasing. "I think I want a boy next time, though. Like Mia, a girl and then a boy. And then maybe another boy, followed by two more girls."

I watched him pale, but instead of arguing, he bent and kissed me. "Whatever you want, baby. As long as you're happy, I'm happy."

I knew he meant it, but I didn't want to put him through this too many more times. I hated seeing him so stressed over my well-being. And there was no telling if the next delivery would actually go as smoothly as this one had.

"Maybe just one or two more," I told him as I covered his left hand, my thumb rubbing over where my name was beautifully inked onto his finger. I would never get tired of seeing his "ring," nor the possessive thrill I got when other women checked him out and he dismissed them with a wave of that hand that showed those bitches that he was mine.

"I think one more couldn't hurt anything," Mom said with a wink at me as she sat on my dad's lap. "After all, you're going to be so busy with all those movies, you don't want to overextend yourself with too many babies right now."

I nodded in agreement, but my eyes lingered on my parents as they cuddled. We didn't talk about what happened with Garon anymore, but I'd made them tell me about what he'd sent them. They refused to tell me what was in the letters he'd left Mom, not wanting to put even more disturbing images in my head.

After Garon was shot, Detective Kirtner took a forensic team to his house and found further proof that he was, in fact, my stalker. Not only had there been a cage full of the poor little birds he'd sent me in some of the packages, but there had been bottles of my favorite lotion beside his bed, along with pictures of me all over his bedroom wall.

Pictures that he'd taken with his phone at a distance or gotten from the camera in my dressing room, which were of me naked while I was changing clothes.

Kirtner had discovered that Garon had a therapist and, after speaking to the man, told us Garon had started losing touch with reality following the death of his father. Garon had never told the man about what he was doing to Mom or me, but the majority of their therapy sessions had been about Garon complaining about Pop-Pop not loving him enough and leaving all his assets to Mom and her children.

Crazily enough, Garon had left me everything in his own will. I guess in his fucked-up mind, he thought we were going to be together forever once he kidnapped me. I hadn't wanted any of his money. It felt tainted and dirty. I donated it to an organization that helped victims of abuse and stalkers start over.

The stake he owned in Strive, however, I'd gifted to Jordan. Now he didn't need to go through Winston Cline to do the supervillainess movies he wanted to franchise. I couldn't wait to lose the twenty pounds I'd gained while pregnant so we could start filming the first movie.

The story of how Garon died and why had caused a huge media frenzy for a few weeks, but once it calmed down, life had gotten back to normal for us. I didn't hold it against my parents for keeping anything from me, and they hadn't done the same with me. We were all at fault, but we'd only been trying to protect one another.

Jordan stroked my hair back from my face, pulling me out of my head. "You are, without a doubt, the most beautiful woman I've ever seen," he murmured, touching his lips to mine. "We can have as many babies as you want, my love. I'll suck it up and deal. I did promise you we would fill up our house, and I still want that too. Just give me a few weeks to recover from being scared something might happen to you."

"Deal," I quickly agreed.

And that was how we ended up needing to add a few bedrooms to our house...

PLAYLIST

"Feel It" by Michele Morrone
    "My Arms" by LEDGER
    "Time After Time" by GUNSHIP
    "Starving" by Hailee Steinfeld & Grey
    "Wait for Me" by From Ashes to New
    "Don't Let Me Down" by Fame on Fire & Arcaeus
    "Listen to Your Heart" by Through Fire
    "Crystalline" by Amaranthe
    "Naked" by Ava Max
    "My Oasis" by Sam Smith (ft. Burna Boy)
    "Me Because of You" by HRVY
    "Shh...Don't Say It" by FLETCHER

Printed in Great Britain
by Amazon